HYPERSPACE HIGH

THE SCHOOL THAT'S OUT OF THIS WORLD

Hyperspace High is first published in the United States by
Stone Arch Books
A Capstone imprint
1710 Roe Crest Drive
North Mankato, Minnesota 56003
www.capstonepub.com

First published in 2013 by Curious Fox
an imprint of Capstone Global Library Limited,
7 Pilgrim Street, London, EC4V 6LB
Registered company number: 6695582
www.curious-fox.com

Text © Hothouse Fiction Ltd 2013
Series created by Hothouse Fiction
www.hothousefiction.com
The author's moral rights are hereby asserted.

Library of Congress Cataloging-in-Publication Data is available on the
Library of Congress website.
ISBN: 978-1-4342-6308-7 (library binding)
ISBN: 978-1-4342-6312-4 (paperback)

Summary: It's competition time at Hyperspace High as the students build
robots to compete in the annual Robot Warriors contest. John and Kaal are in
with a chance of winning, but will competition get in the way of friendship?

Designer: Alison Thiele

With special thanks to Martin Howard

Printed in the United States of America in Stevens Point, Wisconsin.
032013   007227WZF13

ROBOT WARRIORS

written by ZAC HARRISON • illustrated by DANI GEREMIA

STONE ARCH BOOKS™
a capstone imprint   www.capstonepub.com

CHAPTER 1

Walking into Hyperspace High's main lecture hall, John Riley thought for a moment that the colossal ship had vanished around him. As he sat down on a nearby HoloStool, the awesome virtual reality effect of the walls and floor showed the starry heavens scrolling past in perfect 3-D. The black depths of space surrounded the students, dotted with occasional planets and stars. It almost felt as if John could reach out and touch them. However much time he spent on this ship, John never failed to be impressed by his school's technology.

Every single student at Hyperspace High seemed to be in the hall. Students were still crowding in, no two of them alike. They waddled, crawled, fluttered, shuffled, drifted above the ground, or stalked on long, sucker-toed legs.

"Excuse me, human. Can I just squeeze past?"

John looked up at a ten-foot-tall blue slug. "Um . . . sure," John said, with a nervous grin. He drew his legs up on to his MorphSeat and tried to give the creature as much room as he could.

The MorphSeat obligingly changed shape, adapting to his body.

The blue slug squidged past, making a noise like a rubber boot being sucked into mud. It settled itself across two empty MorphSeats with a contented sigh. The seats morphed together into a sort of banana-shaped couch, holding the alien comfortably.

"Thanks," it gurgled.

"No problem," John said, smiling despite his disappointment. He'd been secretly trying to save those seats for his best friends, Emmie and Kaal. But they were nowhere to be seen in the crowd.

More students pressed past John, looking for the few remaining seats — first a greenish, pear-like being with a mouth full of jagged teeth, then something like a round lava lamp that trundled past on tank tracks.

John couldn't help staring in amazement at them. They were just so *alien*.

No, he corrected himself, not *alien*. Just very different from human beings. Even after the weeks he'd spent at Hyperspace High, he still wasn't completely used to it.

All those years he'd spent growing up on Earth, wondering if there might be extraterrestrial life somewhere out among the stars . . . and now here he was, with alien life shoving, elbowing, and — well — *tentacling* him as it crowded past.

Life at a boarding school on Earth would have been a lot less interesting. It was pretty incredible to think about. If he hadn't overslept that fateful morning, jumped onto a suspiciously high-tech bus, and accidentally ended up on Hyperspace High in a Martian prince's place, he'd be back on Earth now.

Of course, his parents thought he *was* there now, which made talking to them about school a bit awkward.

There must be at least a thousand students here, John thought. He could count heads — but that wouldn't be much help, since not every student had a head, and some had several. At any rate, there were *far* more students here than there had been at his old school. What's more, they all seemed excited, as if they were expecting something.

Voices babbled away on all sides.

John felt left out. Nobody had bothered to tell him why they were all gathered in this lecture hall at midday. And he was surprised Kaal and Emmie hadn't come to find him here — they would have told him what was going on. It wasn't a normal assembly, he was sure of that much.

He tried to listen to what the other students were saying and managed to catch a few words:

". . . stomped the Powanator completely flat!"

"Yeah, but then Rippertron pulled its leg off. Not much of a Stomper with only one leg, was it?"

John desperately wanted to ask what they were talking about, but he stopped himself. Plenty of the students already thought he was a "primitive Earthling" who didn't know anything. The last thing he wanted to do was prove them right.

Fortunately, he didn't have to wait long to find out. With a *wheeze-STOMP, wheeze-STOMP* of mechanical limbs, Master Tronic came hulking onto the stage.

Master Tronic wasn't just the technology teacher — he himself was a walking, talking technology class. He liked to rebuild his body depending on what he was teaching the students at any given time.

John rubbed his elbow and winced as he remembered the time Master Tronic had taken the form of a kinetic force cannon to teach them about particle collisions. The rapid-fire zero-G tennis ball barrage had gotten a bit out of hand, and his elbow felt sore just remembering the accident.

Today, Master Tronic was a robot. His upper body was huge and ape-like, armored with metal plates and strung with cables, while his legs ended in two gigantic saucer-shaped feet. He swung his metal skull from left to right, glowering at the students.

John swallowed hard.

Does this mean trouble? he wondered.

Master Tronic began to speak. With each

word, a narrow band of red light throbbed in his skull. His deep electronic voice boomed through the hall. "I am delighted to announce this year's Robot Warriors contest."

A hush fell over the hall. John glanced around and saw all the students excitedly taking notes, whispering to one another, and fidgeting in giddy excitement. Obviously, they all knew what a Robot Warriors contest was and couldn't wait to get started. John guessed he must be the only student in the whole school who had no idea what it was all about. Even so, he had to admit that it sounded cool.

"The rules of the contest," rumbled Master Tronic, "are exactly the same as last year — and indeed every year."

John's heart sank. He had no idea of the rules and dreaded the thought of asking for help, without his friends nearby to tell him.

"However," Master Tronic continued, "I shall go over the rules once again for our first years' benefit. There is NO EXCUSE FOR FORGETTING THEM."

Suddenly, John felt a lot better.

"Each student is to build his or her own robot, and these robots will go on to compete against each other in a series of trials. The trials change every year, but students will not be told what they are ahead of time. However, I can tell you this." Master Tronic leaned forward. "Brute strength alone will NOT be enough to win!"

"Says the teacher built like a battle droid," the slug whispered to John.

"Tomorrow has been chosen as Robot-Building Day," Master Tronic said. "All other classes have been canceled. Instead, you will spend tomorrow designing and building your robots!"

Wild cheers broke out in the hall. Master Tronic waved his hands for calm.

John was the only one who wasn't cheering. He was staring ahead, open-mouthed. *One day?* He had only ONE DAY to design and build a robot?

"As always, the rule is one robot per student. No team entries are allowed, and every student is expected to participate."

Including me, John thought. The thought was terrifying and exciting at the same time.

"The first rounds will be held the day after tomorrow," Master Tronic continued. "Then, the next day, the semi-finals and finals will take place, and the winner will be crowned Robot Warrior Champion of the Year!" He paused. "And although luck is a superstitious concept that has no place in a technology class . . . good luck!"

The students left the hall in a chattering rush. John wandered through the Center, still burning with questions about the contest. Everywhere he looked, from the seats by the rippling lake to the starlit balconies under the great dome, students were talking eagerly about robots and nothing else. It was as if the entire school had gone robot crazy!

John shook his head and kept looking for his friends.

He finally found Kaal and Emmie sitting at a table in Ska's Café, in a far corner where the black walls swirled with nebular patterns. Kaal, John's roommate from the planet Derril, had crammed his huge, green demon-like body behind the table, as if he was hiding behind it. Beside him, the beautiful Sillaran, Emmie, was waving excitedly. The most human-looking of any of the other pupils on Hyperspace High,

Emmie's faintly golden skin shone and her navy-blue eyes twinkled brightly as she beckoned John over.

John navigated past tables crowded with feathered and diamond-scaled beings, tables where students were already building little model robots out of drinking straws and alien cutlery.

Emmie pushed back her chair and bounded up to him, her gleaming, silver hair trailing like rocket exhaust. "Can you believe it?" she asked, smiling widely. "It's Robot Warriors time already! What are you going to make? Have you decided yet?"

"I'm . . . uh . . . still at the design stage," John said quickly.

"Smart move!" croaked Gyrim Florm, a frog-like, midnight-black third-year student with a white mohawk of hair and a silver kilt who sat at the next table over. "Check out the competition first, THEN decide! I like your style."

"I'm going to build Thunderbolt Three," said his companion, Bosquip, who was mostly tentacles and a single goggling eye. "Loads of armor and an electron ram. Like last year's robot — only better."

"That's what you said last year," Gyrim pointed out. "When you built Thunderbolt Two, and it exploded."

"It still lasted longer than Thunderbolt One," Bosquip said stubbornly.

"Which holds the record for the shortest-lived robot in the history of the contest," Emmie said brightly.

"What happened?" John had to ask.

Gyrim hesitated. "It aimed, it fired . . . and it blew a great big hole in the hull. *Whoosh*, it got sucked out into space. Lasted three whole seconds."

"Three *glorious* seconds!" Bosquip said with a sigh, quivering his tentacles dramatically. Everyone laughed, even John.

A robo-waiter glided over to them, bringing a transparent tray with three tall purple glasses.

"Brucko juices are on me," Emmie said. "Good luck, everyone!"

As the three of them leaned in to slurp at their drinks, John said in a low voice to Emmie and Kaal, "What's the big deal with this contest, anyway? Everyone's going crazy over it."

Emmie's blue eyes went very wide. "You don't know?"

"Of course he doesn't know," Kaal whispered. "He's *new*."

John sucked at his Brucko juice. His mouth flooded with amazing flavor — sweet and zingy at the same time, like plum and cherry syrup with exploding pop rocks in it.

"Suck the bubbles up," Emmie told him. "They're chewy."

John chased bubbles around with his straw while Kaal did his best to explain the contest.

"Winning the Robot Warriors contest is basically a shortcut to being king or queen of the school," the giant Derrilian said. "You get major respect from all the students. Everyone wants to be your friend. And there's a prize."

"The prize is always *epic*," said Emmie, through a mouthful of bubbles.

"Hey, check out Quondass val Haq," said Kaal. "He won the contest last year. Now look at him."

Quondass was a scaly-bodied student with a round belly and fangs like broom handles that jutted from his lower lip. He reminded John of a troll figure he'd once painted for a war game. As usual, Quondass had his fan club around him, a gang of adoring students who kept his table supplied with drinks and snacks. As John watched, the whole group laughed loudly at the same time.

"His jokes aren't even funny," Emmie said, "but they all laugh anyway."

Aha! John thought. *He won! Well, that explains why he's so popular! I always wondered about that. I mean, I guess it couldn't have been for his amazing good looks or sense of humor. . . .*

"So they still think he's awesome, even a year later?"

"Oh, yeah, definitely," Emmie said. "You see, his prize was a private gig by Neutron Decay, the heaviest heavy rock band in the entire galaxy! All those fans of his are students he put on the guest list!"

"Wow," John said. "So what's this year's prize?"

"Nobody knows," Kaal said. "But the funny thing is — it's always something the winner really wants. As if *someone* knew who would win, before the contest even started!"

John and Emmie looked at one another. "Lorem," they said at the same time. Lorem, Hyperspace High's headmaster, had the ability to see into the future.

"So what would you want to be the prize if you won, Emmie?" Kaal asked, finishing his Brucko juice with a loud slurp.

"A new model Flitter X5000," Emmie answered instantly.

"What's wrong with your old one?" John joked.

Emmie had shown him clips of her flying her little personal ship back home on Sillar, weaving quickly in between trees at high, dangerous speeds.

"Nothing's *wrong* with it. It just doesn't have the cool lights underneath, or the turbo button, or the underwater cruising mode. So, what would *you* want the prize to be, Kaal?" Emmie asked.

"Nothing much," Kaal said mildly. "Just a trip home over break. I mean, I know we'll get to go back home at the end of the semester, but —"

"*But* the poor Derrilian is all homesick," sneered a familiar arrogant voice. "What's the matter, Kaal? Missing your mommy?"

Everyone turned to look. Mordant Talliver had crept up behind them. Above his shoulder hovered his constant companion and only friend, the tennis-ball-sized droid, G-Vez. "Oh, that was a good one, master," it chirped.

Mordant's yellow eyes gleamed as the black rubbery tentacles that grew from his ribcage rubbed together in delight. The half-Gargon never missed an opportunity to bully his classmates, and his silver drone was always quick to praise his efforts.

"Why don't you enter that Serve-U-Droid of yours in the contest?" John asked. "There might be a boot-licking round."

"We have to design our own robots from scratch. Surely even *you* know that," Mordant said nastily, as he swung back his large mane of black hair. "I wouldn't even bother trying if I were you. Your primitive human brain doesn't stand a chance!"

G-Vez agreed. "Quite so, master. Perhaps the Earthling will try to make a robot out of sticks and animal skins!"

Mordant gave a low laugh

G-Vez bobbed up and down.

"Get lost, Talliver," Emmie said.

"Don't worry, I'm going. I've got to get started on my winning design," Mordant said, and scurried away. One of his tentacles flicked the back of John's head in a final insulting salute.

"You know, I don't much care who wins, so long as it isn't *him*," Kaal muttered, as soon as Mordant was out of sight.

But John wasn't listening. He was lost in his own thoughts.

He wasn't just going to enter the Robot Warriors contest.

Now he wanted to *win* it.

No prize could be better than showing the likes of Mordant Talliver that a "primitive Earthling" really did deserve to be a student at Hyperspace High.

In fact, John thought it might prove to the

whole school that he was just as entitled to be a student here as everyone else.

This was his chance.

CHAPTER 2

"Good morning!" boomed Master Tronic. "Welcome to a whole day of technology class!"

The first-year students whooped and cheered.

"I will be checking in on things from room to room, so Ms. Skrinel has kindly agreed to supervise you in my absence, with the help of this Examiner."

The white, egg-shaped Examiner stood blank-faced. Examiners were on the spaceship to maintain discipline and order, using their scanners to quickly determine violations and punish students accordingly.

John's first encounter with the Examiners happened just minutes after landing on Hyperspace High. He had been classified as an intruder and was almost ejected into outer space. If it hadn't been for Lorem coming to the rescue just in time and offering John a chance to stay at the school, John's body would be forever spiraling in the depths of the galaxy.

John winced at the memory and then winced again at the sight of Ms. Skrinel. The Cosmic Languages teacher looked like a pink snake oozing with white slime. Her tail ended in a bright-yellow, upward-pointing dart, which she often used to point at things on the screen. She was never purposely rude, but she did have a tendency to spray gunk over you when she talked.

At least this wasn't a Cosmic Languages class. John wasn't crazy about those. Mimicking the speech of species with mandibles or beaks was difficult, and even if he could, he wasn't sure why he'd ever need to. The ship's computer automatically translated everything anyway. Otherwise, he'd never have been able to understand a word anyone was saying.

"I will not sssstand for any ssssilliness or ssslacking from the sssstudents!" Ms. Skrinel said, spattering the front row of desks. The students groaned.

Master Tronic went on. "You may discuss your projects with your fellow students in class, since you will undoubtedly do so *out* of class," he said. Everyone chuckled. "You may even help one another, if you choose." Master Tronic's head pulsed with its sinister red light. "But there is to be NO COPYING. Stealing another student's ideas will result in immediate disqualification."

"NO COPYING, OTHERWISE IMMEDIATE DISQUALIFICATION," the Examiner repeated.

"Is that clear?"

"Yes sir," John replied with the rest of the class.

"You have until eight o'clock this evening to finish your robots. At that time, all completed robots will be taken by the Examiners and placed in safe storage. All unfinished robots will be destroyed."

There was an ominous pause.

"Begin!" declared Master Tronic, and stomped out of the room.

Immediately, a handful of students leaped up from their desks and charged over to the Junkyard, the technology storage room where useful bits and pieces were kept. They emerged soon afterwards, clutching armfuls of struts, springs, casings, and wire. In virtually no time at all, they had already begun welding them together with micro-laser tools.

John stared at them, awed that the other students found this all so easy. He hadn't even begun yet and was already starting to doubt his ability to win — or even complete — the competition.

The other students all seemed to be certain of what they were looking for, and how they would build, mold, and weld in order to make a functioning robot. Where on Earth would *he* start?

John looked around. The students who weren't already welding had fired up their desk-coms and were beginning to design their robots carefully. Kaal was using a sensor interface to design what looked like a pair of wings. As he moved his hands gracefully, his desk-com traced the lines of movement, sculpting objects in 3-D.

John had no idea what to do or where to start.

But that's what friends are for, he thought.

He nudged Kaal with his elbow, hoping to ask him for help, but in doing so, he knocked Kaal's steady hand.

"Sorry!" John said quickly, but his best friend still turned and glared at him.

A little taken aback at Kaal's reaction, John chastised himself for interrupting his friend. *That was really dumb*, he thought. *I know how important this is to Kaal.*

He looked down and studied the screen on his own personal desk-com. It showed diagrams of different robot components and how they worked.

Perhaps this was simpler than he had imagined. Could he just pick different components and then put them together?

"Maybe it's just like getting a box of LEGOs for Christmas," he said to himself.

But the more he looked, the more complicated it seemed. He'd never thought about how many different decisions you had to make in building a robot. For example, a robot could move about on wheels, treads, legs, or even float on a levitation field. It could see with camera eyes, or scan with sonar, or peer into the sub-etheric spectrum. It could have arms, or extensible tools, or a manipulation field like the Examiners had.

John shook his head in frustration. It was like the candy section at the local supermarket back in his hometown on Earth; there were just way too many choices!

John was already starting to feel anxious. He wanted to prove himself in this competition! He glanced over to where Emmie was sitting. Her face was screwed up in concentration as she worked, determined to do her best. That made him feel a bit better. At least he wasn't the only one finding it difficult. Unlike technology-whiz Kaal, Emmie struggled with most academic subjects.

Kaal must have seen the look on Emmie's face, too. He left his desk and went over to Emmie. "Don't look at the bits and try to make something out of them," he suggested to her. "Come up with a design first, then pick out the bits you need to make it."

Emmie looked like a lightbulb had suddenly switched on over her head. "Thanks, Kaal!" she said.

"Of course," John said, grinning. When you

looked at it that way, it seemed much easier. He scratched his head and focused his mind on a possible design.

Maybe a huge hand that could crawl around on its fingers and curl into a fist to bash things?

But then he realized a hand would need an arm to do that, and an arm needed a shoulder, and so on. Well, he could always just do a human-shaped robot — but that was too obvious, and Mordant would laugh his tentacles off at John's lack of imagination.

He needed to *think outside the box*, as his dad sometimes said.

What about a huge spinning-top-like robot? No — that was too babyish. He might as well put flowers and bunny rabbits on it.

John doodled on his desk-com screen, wishing an idea would just jump into his head. All around him, students were busily working away. The student on his right was designing a robot like a soccer ball, which could hover on an air cushion and ricochet off the walls. The one on his left was designing a smooth, white android with a dark visor and blades at the end of its arms.

Now *that* was a cool robot. John wished he'd thought of it. The designs all seemed pretty obvious once he'd seen others come up with them.

"How on Earth am I supposed to compete with them?" John muttered to himself. The other students had all grown up with working robots, reprogrammed robots, or built robots of their own. They were as common as household pets everywhere except on primitive Earth, it seemed.

The only robot John had ever built had been made out of yogurt containers and pipe cleaners, when he was six. It definitely didn't do anything.

Master Tronic had said they were allowed to help each other. Now that Kaal had finished his design, John wondered if he should try to ask him again for help — or Emmie, perhaps. But the more he thought about it, the worse he felt. It wasn't fair to distract his friends from their own robots, just because he didn't have a clue.

Then a thought struck him. Had Master Tronic been looking at *him* when he said that? Did he expect the primitive Earthling to *need* help? No.

I am going to do this myself, John decided. If the other students could design a robot, then so could he. He just needed an idea. He sat chewing his stylus and thinking hard.

Ms. Skrinel came slithering down between the rows of desks. Her beady eyes were fixed on John. "May I ask why you are just ssssitting there, ssssstaring into sssspace?" she demanded. Every "s" sent a spray of goo over his desk-com. "Everyone elssssse is working hard! Sssshow me your design, please."

"I haven't actually come up with one yet," he admitted, trying to keep his voice down.

"Then I ssssuggest you get on with it," Ms. Skrinel told him frostily. "Although the contessssst is meant to be —" she made a disapproving face at the word — "*fun*, it sssstill countssss as part of your technology classsses! Every student needs to make a robot, John Riley. The Examiners have punishments in sssstore for those who don't!"

She slithered away. John took a tissue and carefully wiped the slime off his desk-com. "No pressure, then," he grumbled to himself.

John refreshed the screen on his desk-com,

determined to make a start. But first, he had another quick look around to see what the other students were doing. Maybe their ideas would spark something in his mind.

Lishtig ar Steero came out of the Junkyard, wheeling a huge bundle of purple nano-fibers, like fine phosphorescent hair, on a hover-trolley. Matching the color of his own hair, the purple mass looked like he had sprouted a twin. He sat back down at his desk and began flinging clumps of fiber everywhere. It soon looked like a Lishtig bomb had gone off.

Kaal's robotic wings were slowly taking shape. A chunky, holographic model of them now floated above his desk-com, moving in a simulated airflow.

Many students were still at the design stage, painstakingly assembling their robots on-screen before building anything, but more and more were now rummaging about in the Junkyard, coming out with strange, dangerous-looking gizmos and bits of salvaged electronics. Lishtig was welding fistfuls of purple hair onto his robot. Even Emmie was designing in earnest now, molding some sort of shimmering plastic skin around a framework. The skin changed colors as John watched.

Come on, he thought, *you have to think of something!*

In desperation, John thought of childhood toys. He sketched a robot that would move by *boinging* on one huge spring foot. The computer ran a simulation for him, showing his robot ricocheting off the walls and ceiling, bashing itself to pieces.

"Oh, yeah," John said to himself. "That's a winner."

He cleared the screen and started again.

Maybe something that isn't a huge robotic body part? he thought.

* * *

By the time the bell sounded for lunch, he had discarded three more useless ideas.

Steamroller X would have been good at squishing things, but it was obviously based on "primitive" Earth technology, and students like Mordant would have mocked him once they'd found out.

Blobbo the Blobby, a robot made of absorbent Devouro-Gel, wasn't technically a robot at all, as it had no mechanical parts and got auto-banned by the desk-com, at which point the Examiner had zoomed over and delivered a surprisingly stern warning about not using school property to engage in intergalactic weapons research.

And the less said about Cornettron the ice-cream cone, the better.

John felt depressed. Perhaps he really *couldn't* make the grade at Hyperspace High after all. Certainly not if this morning's efforts were anything to go by.

John joined the throng of students heading out into the hallway. With his hands thrust deep into his pockets, he scowled at them all. They all chatted excitedly about their stupid robots.

He looked up to see Emmie's head bobbing along in front, the huge form of Kaal beside her.

Had they forgotten to wait for John? Were they embarrassed by their stupid Earthling friend today?

John tried to shake the paranoid thought from his head, just as he heard two students behind him, deep in conversation.

"So, are you going with a plasmic power core, or a neutrino nexus?" John heard one of them say.

"Neither," the other replied. "He has a separate power core in each limb. That way he can break into five parts and then come back together again!"

"Aargh! Why didn't I think of that?"

"Maybe because your dad doesn't own a robot design company?"

The two students strolled past John without giving him a second glance. John clenched his jaw.

"I'm not going to give up," he told himself under his breath. "Who cares if I'm not a galactic genius like all the rest of them? All sorts of brilliant inventors came from Earth!" He struggled to think of some as he walked. "There's that Dyson guy . . . and Steve Jobs, and Alexander Graham Bell . . . and, uh, that man who invented Stevenson's Rocket — what was his name again . . ."

John had planned to get some lunch, but when he saw the number of students heading towards the Center, he changed his mind and walked towards his dorm instead. They'd all want to chat about *their* robots, and he'd had enough of that. What he needed now was some peace and quiet, so he could come up with some ideas of his own.

The TravelTube was cool, quiet, and empty. John leaned into a corner of the elevator-like transport cubicle as it began to sink. He felt tired already, and the day had barely begun.

A shimmering ball of light slowly rose through the TravelTube's floor. It hovered in front of John and morphed itself into the shape of Lorem, the headmaster.

"It's not like you to miss lunch," Lorem said. His voice was kind, with an edge of concern.

"I'm not very hungry."

"Is something bothering you, John Riley?" Lorem asked.

John scuffed his foot into the floor, and he took a deep breath. "Yeah, to be honest, it is," he said quietly. "It's the Robot Warriors contest. I don't know where to start, what to make. I guess . . . I just feel really out of my depth with it, you know?"

Lorem frowned. "I see. I am afraid the blame lies with me, my young friend."

"With *you*? I don't get it."

"It was my belief that an Earthling could flourish at Hyperspace High, even among more advanced races. I thought it was best to include everyone if I could, despite the differences in their backgrounds. Spread the message of our school far and wide! But we do have to face facts. Earth's technology has a long way to go to catch up with the other planets, no matter how brilliant individual Earthlings may be."

"I've done okay up to now, I guess," John said carefully, not wanting to hurt Lorem's feelings. "But this contest's really tough. I've never done anything like it before."

"I understand. I'm sorry, John Riley. The challenges we set are meant to encourage the students, not humiliate them. If this school is asking too much of you, then we should perhaps think of other options."

"You think I should go back to Earth?" John said miserably.

"That is up to you," Lorem said gently. "I just want you to know that you *can*. Nobody would think any less of you if you did, I assure you."

John thought of Mordant Talliver sneering in triumph. But then, if he were back on Earth, he'd never have to see the half-Gargon bully again. So what would it matter?

"Think about it," Lorem said.

Suddenly he was a twinkling ball of light again. The ball wafted up through the TravelTube ceiling, leaving John alone with his thoughts. Lorem's out-of-the-blue suggestion had surprised and confused him.

Was leaving Hyperspace High really the best thing to do?

CHAPTER 3

The door to John's dorm room hummed open. He threw himself into a chair, which immediately billowed up to receive him.

"Hi there!" rang the disembodied voice of the ship's computer system, which first John — and now the rest of the students — had taken to calling Zepp.

"Hi," said John bleakly.

"I think I detect negative brainwaves. Is my favorite Earthling out of sorts today?" Zepp asked kindly.

"Hrmph," John replied. He folded his arms on the table in front of him and sank his head onto them.

"Okay," the computer said, sounding serious now. "You aren't acting like your usual self. Something's wrong, isn't it?"

John raised his head and let out a long, slow sigh. "I'm finished, defeated, game over!" he said. "I can't come up with an idea for a robot, let alone build one. And now Lorem thinks I should go home to Earth. He thinks he was wrong to keep me on Hyperspace High. He doesn't think I'm up to it."

Zepp made an electronic whistling noise. "I can understand why you're upset. That must be hard for you."

"Thanks," said John.

"Though you shouldn't be too tough on yourself," Zepp said, instantly perking up again.

"You haven't even been here for a full semester! Thirty-three days and four hours, to be precise. Most of the other students have made many, many robots before."

"I suppose you're right," John said, still feeling unsure.

"But, listen. It's actually not that difficult to design a robot, not with the software I've got installed. You don't have to worry about all the fiddly electronic details. That's for advanced classes; it's a long way off yet. All you have to do is make a sketch or two using your desk-com and program your demands for the robot's capabilities into the computer. By choosing various options and picking your materials, it'll do the rest!"

"But don't we have to *build* the robots?" John asked.

"You have to assemble them," Zepp said.

"The computer makes the different parts out of the stuff that you find. You just provide the materials and the design, and put the pieces together."

It's like putting together a model kit, John thought. He felt some of the weight lift from his shoulders. *Maybe this won't be so bad.*

The thought of assembling models reminded John of his bedroom back on Earth. He suddenly missed his parents. Maybe it was a good time to give them a call.

"Zepp, could you check to see if my mom's online?"

"Yes, she is!" Zepp almost trilled. "Right now she's looking at a discussion thread on MomsNet about someone called George Clooney, who apparently suffers from critical overheating. How fascinating! Do many humans become 'super hot?'"

"Just make the call, please," John said. He hastily bundled up all the Holo-comics, Derrilian snack boxes, and vid crystals that lay around the room. He couldn't risk giving his mum the slightest clue that he wasn't safely tucked away at boarding school.

It wasn't long before his mother's surprised, delighted face appeared on the wall screen.

"John! How lovely to hear from you, darling! How have you been?"

"Pretty good," John said, and immediately felt a thousand times better. "Still getting used to things, you know. But it's fun. I miss you and Dad, though."

"We miss you too, dear!" She sighed and glanced around the room. "Your dad's at work, of course. He won't be back till six o'clock at the earliest. But I'm sure he'd send his love if he were here."

John frowned. "Are you all right, Mom?"

"Oh, don't worry about me, John. It's just . . . with you off at boarding school and your dad at work all day, I'm rattling around this big old empty house all on my own. It does get lonely, I have to admit. So I've been thinking about adding a new member to the family."

John's eyes widened. He was an only child and thought his parents were happy with it that way.

"Another kid?" he asked.

"A dog!" she said, laughing at his expression. "You remember Mrs. Weirzbowski from up the road? She works for a dog-rescue charity now, and she says there's this one little Jack Russell who'd be perfect for our house. Your dad says he'd rather have one of those Weimaraners, goes on about how noble they look, but I couldn't cope with something that big. I'd live in fear of it knocking my china hedgehogs off the shelf. So, what do you think?"

"Mom, that would be *amazing*!" John said. He'd always wanted a dog.

"And you wouldn't mind a Jack Russell? I always thought you'd want something huge and hairy, like your father does."

"Seriously, Mom, a Jack Russell would rock. I can't wait to meet it."

John thought that it was a shame he'd have to wait until the end of the semester to meet the dog. But then, as he said goodbye to his mom, an idea came to him.

An *awesome* idea.

The more he thought about it, the more awesome it was. And best of all, nobody else on Hyperspace High could have thought of it.

John allowed himself a little smile of relief. Perhaps he wasn't a lost cause after all.

* * *

Back in the technology lab, John got down to work. With only half a day left, he was working frantically, with hardly a pause for breath.

The design steadily took shape on his desk-com. Once he'd explained to the computer what a "dog" was and grabbed some images of Jack Russells from Earth's internet for reference, the rest had been easy. Just as easy as Zepp had predicted. The computer-generated mock-up of his robot dog barked and wagged its tail. It had a visor instead of eyes and its body was covered in metal plates, but it was still just a dog at this stage. John thought it looked pretty cool.

"You need some special features," John said to it. "Computer, can you give him a homing system? I want him to find his way back whenever he's called."

"Confirmed," the computer said. The robotic dog's ears vanished, and long antennae appeared in their place. At the same time, the computer image showed a black cylinder inside his stomach.

"Great," John said. "I want him to fly, too. Add a rocket booster."

A rocket pipe appeared, sticking out of the dog's bottom.

"Not there!" John said. "Okay — better make it two rocket boosters, one on each side of his body."

The computer changed the design, and the new design was a huge improvement. Now he needed weapons — and what better weapon for a dog than razor-sharp teeth?

John smiled. "Computer, replace his teeth with metal ones. As sharp as you can make them. I want teeth that can rip through armor!"

With a popping sound like popcorn, the teeth appeared one by one. Suddenly, the robot dog looked fearsome, but still somehow cute. John grinned. This was starting to be fun. He quickly hit the Save button, thinking proudly of how much work he'd put in already, in such a short span of time.

"Still not finished?" a voice interrupted. "Why are you losers even bothering?" It was Mordant Talliver. "I'd give up now if I were you. You don't have a chance."

John glanced up, annoyed, but Mordant wasn't talking to him — at least, not *only* to him. He was sauntering down between the desks, with G-Vez hovering over one shoulder and a freshly built cone-shaped robot about half his height following behind.

It emitted a low, sinister hum.

Around him, students continued to work on

their robots. No one bothered to look Mordant in the eye.

Trust Mordant Talliver to turn a fun contest into a game of I'm-better-than-you, John thought ruefully.

Not so long ago, Mordant had nearly gotten into major trouble by running away during a school trip, until it was revealed he'd been brainwashed by a sinister alien warlord. John got the distinct impression that Mordant had been humiliated by the brainwashing incident and was determined to boost his reputation by winning the contest.

"Of course he finished first," G-Vez crooned. "Master is by far the most talented student in the whole class."

"Check out my robot," Mordant said. "This is IFI."

"Looks *iffy* to me all right," John muttered. He wished Ms. Skrinel would finish whatever she was dealing with in the Junkyard and come and supervise like she was supposed to. Mordant's antics often ended in trouble — usually with John as the target.

"I bet you're wondering what it stands for!" Mordant went on.

"Not particularly," Emmie said, without looking up.

Mordant scowled at her. "It means Invincible For Infinity!" He pressed a control, and a set of spindly arms in a ring extended from halfway up the robot. "Eight arms, each one with a needler pistol! Hoverpad to move about on! And don't even think about trying to attack it. Know why?" Nobody in the group seemed to want to know why.

Mordant angrily grabbed G-Vez out of the air, making him bleep with surprise. He threw the tiny Serve-U-Droid hard at IFI.

G-Vez rebounded off an invisible force field and whizzed off towards the ceiling. He righted himself and came flying back, a little wobbly, towards his master.

"Most inventive, sir!" he babbled. "A force shield defense. Master, I believe IFI will be unstoppable!"

Unstoppable, huh? We'll see about that, John thought.

"Computer, make the tail into a blade," he said quietly. "I want it to hit hard when other robots least expect it!"

The computer obeyed. The dog's little tail was replaced with a flexible jointed blade like a sword made of segments. According to the data on the screen, it could slice through reinforced plasteel.

"Wow," John whispered.

"What's that supposed to be?" said a nasty

voice. Mordant had quietly slithered up behind him.

"Nothing you'd ever have heard of," John said, without turning around.

Mordant leaned in close and whispered in his ear. "Let's get one thing straight between us. I am going to win this competition, or there's going to be trouble."

"Whatever," John said with a shrug, but his stomach was turning cartwheels.

When Mordant Talliver made a threat like that, you could be sure he meant it. He had a knack for getting other people into trouble just so he could watch them flounder. And even when Mordant broke school rules himself, he always managed to wriggle out of the punishment somehow.

To John's relief, suddenly Master Tronic came clanking over toward them.

Mordant retreated with a final warning hiss.

"How are you doing, Mr. Riley?" Master Tronic asked.

"Much better now, thanks," John said.

Master Tronic scanned the desk-com with glimmering eye-lasers and nodded in approval. "Your design's coming along well, I see. But you still need to choose your materials."

"I haven't had time yet!" John protested, his anxiety slipping back. "I've never done this before. I —"

Master Tronic held up a robotic hand. "Steady now! Many of your classmates have never built a robot before, either, as first-year students. That's why I'm here — to help. Can I recommend beronzium for the teeth?"

John blinked. "Beronzi-what?"

"It's a metal used in heavy-duty cutting equipment. There's an old battle droid in the

Junkyard with a beronzium claw. You can recycle that if you like."

"Brilliant!" John said, taking notes.

"And for the homing device, perhaps you could reuse the navigation system core from one of our old deep-space probes. . . ."

By the time Master Tronic had finished, John had made a lengthy shopping list of materials. He felt inspired — and a million times more confident than before. He was more certain than ever that he could do this project.

But there were only four hours left on the clock! He'd just have to hope that it was long enough to turn his design into a fully assembled robot.

At least the design was complete . . . except for one thing. John tapped the blank section labeled PROJECT NAME, and entered the words SUPER-ROVER.

Now for the materials, John thought.

He headed over to the Junkyard, taking a deep breath as he looked over the huge stacks and shelves full of electronic components and weird-looking bits of technology from all different planets.

Fortunately, Master Tronic had told him which bins and drawers to look in, and it wasn't too long before he was guiding a hover-trolley laden with junk towards his desk.

"Hi, John!" Emmie called as she came his way. "Check these out!"

Something was moving next to her, a hovering object like a disc with a flat underside and two stubby vertical tail fins. It blended in with the desks and the floor, as if it were made of translucent glass.

Also next to Emmie was a figure in a bubble-like helmet, its head uncannily like a dolphin's.

She was a P'Sidion, John remembered — one of the first aliens he'd met. Her robot was hovering in the air beside her, a single long tentacle of steel with tiny sharp teeth and a crackling blue tip to its tail.

John whistled. "Nice robots!"

"This is Cammy," Emmie explained. "Cammy, visible mode!"

The hovering disc's skin changed to a dull silver, and now John could see it clearly. "Camouflage, huh?" he said, impressed. "Wait a minute. Cammy looks kind of like a miniature Flitter X5000. . . ."

"I thought it might be lucky,' Emmie said, laughing. "And check out Dol's robot!"

"This is Electric E!" Dol said proudly. The hovering eel-like robot buzzed and clicked threateningly. "Don't worry. He's very well trained."

"Glad to hear it," John said, steering well clear of the sparking tail. "Look, I'd love to chat, but . . ."

"Of course, you still have to finish your robot!" Emmie shooed him off toward his desk. "Go on, then! Hurry up. We'll catch up with you later!"

John sat down at his work station and rubbed his hands together. Finally, it was time to build his —

He stared. The desk-com's screen was completely blank.

Frantically, John typed "Super-Rover" into the keyboard.

The desk-com replied with a tiny, blinking message that read:

PROJECT NOT FOUND.

Cold horror crept over him.

He punched the RELOAD PROJECT

icon, but the computer just flashed up a single message:

PROJECT DELETED.

CHAPTER 4

Right on cue, Mordant Talliver came sidling over.

"What's wrong, John Riley? It looks like you're having a bit of trouble with your computer."

"Mind your own business," John said, too angry to think of anything more clever.

"How's your design coming along?" Mordant asked.

This time, John didn't say anything at all.

Mordant shook his head. "Oops. Looks like

you've wiped it. Clumsy. I bet you pressed the wrong icon."

"I don't know why they let a primitive try to use one of these sophisticated desk-coms," added G-Vez.

"I'm surprised he didn't try to worship it as a god," said Mordant. "Too bad, human. Better luck in next year's contest."

Mordant chuckled to himself as he walked away.

You did this, Mordant, I know it, John thought furiously.

He was certain of it. Those long Gargon tentacles could easily have slithered under the desk-coms and fiddled with his console. John realized he had been an easy target for Mordant — too focused and out of his comfort zone to have time to think about protecting his work from the class bully.

But no one had been standing nearby to see it. He had no proof. And even if he had, his work was still gone.

There was only one person on the whole ship who could help him now — and it wasn't even a person.

"Zepp," John said under his breath. "Can you hear me? I need your help!"

"Affirmative," said the computer, talking through the desk-com speaker. "I'm wired into every device on this ship!"

"Can you restore a deleted file? My robot project's been wiped!"

"Let me see . . ." Zepp said. There was a pause. Then the computer said, "This is not good. All the local data's been deleted. I will assess my archives. I might be able to piece it back together."

"Please try!" John's hands trembled with

worry. All that work, ruined. And for nothing more than sheer spite.

The seconds seemed like hours as John waited for Zepp to respond.

"Good news, John Riley! The files are fragmented, but recoverable! Give me five minutes, and Super-Rover will be back with you!"

"Zepp, you rock," John said, sinking onto his desk in relief. "Wow. I seriously owe you big for this."

There was a tap on his shoulder. It was Kaal, looking worried.

"What in the nine moons was *that* all about?" he asked, gesturing at Mordant's back.

"I can't prove it," John whispered, "but I'm pretty sure Mordant deleted my whole project. Zepp's recovering the files, but it's taking time. Time I don't have."

"He just can't resist, can he?" Kaal glanced in disgust at the gloating boy, who was taking his robot, IFI, on another tour of the classroom. "Seriously, if I were you, I'd report him to Master Tronic."

"For cheating?" John said. "That's way worse than just copying. They might even expel him for that. You know what the Examiners are like."

"You know, they just might," Kaal said with a dark look. "Wouldn't that be a shame, if Mordant got kicked out? Can't you just picture the look on his face?"

John thought about it. "I don't think so. I've got less than four hours left to build Super-Rover as it is," he said. "I don't want to waste any more time."

"They'd give you an extension. You know they would!"

John knew Kaal was right.

But if Mordant gets expelled, he thought, *I won't have a chance to show him up in the contest. And I really, really want to beat him.*

"It's tempting," he admitted. "But you know what would be even better? Beating him fair and square."

Just then, Zepp interrupted with a triumphant, tinny fanfare. "Good news! All project files successfully recovered!"

"Better let you get to work, then," Kaal said, smiling. "Cool-looking robot, by the way."

"Thanks!"

John grinned. It was a huge relief to see Super-Rover's schematics spread out in front of him again — every servo, wire, and circuit in place. He was doubly relieved that Kaal seemed to be back to his usual, friendly self.

Ms. Skrinel said this was supposed to be fun, John

thought. *But I see now that it's much more serious than that. In fact, it looks like some people don't care how many rules they break, as long as it helps them win. I thought people would play fair. I won't make that mistake again.*

John got to work.

The electronic chime rang out, telling him it was six o'clock.

Only two hours left? John thought desperately. *But it was five o'clock just a moment ago!*

Super-Rover was slowly but surely taking shape. John had given him a metal skeleton made from recycled struts, and his homing-device power core had been strapped in place inside his belly. The socket for the tail was installed and the tail was even going to be able to wag. He didn't have a head yet, but John was still really proud of him.

Master Tronic stepped to the front of the

class. "You are dismissed for half an hour to go and get some dinner!" he boomed. "Remember, robots can go without food. Organic beings cannot."

"And even if we could, who'd want to?" Lishtig said, laughing. "Come on, guys. I'm starving."

John's stomach gave a tell-tale rumble. There was still so much to do, and he didn't want to waste any more time. Some of the other students continued to work, skipping their evening meal so they could finish their robots. He wondered if he should do the same.

No. He'd skipped lunch already. If he didn't eat, he'd fall over.

"Zepp, can you lock my console? I'm worried that Mordant might try to delete my work again."

"Consider it done," Zepp beeped. "And

don't worry about Super-Rover. I'll put him in a stasis field to protect against sabotage. Now, what would you like to request for dinner? I've been researching several new Earth dishes today!"

"Maybe we should just stick to grilled cheese," John said. He didn't want to risk having Zepp make something that might not turn out right — he didn't have time for trying over.

"Understood! And I've got a surprise that'll go *perfectly* with those sandwiches! Something you previously asked me to develop . . ."

Emmie and Kaal were waiting at their usual spot in the cafeteria. John's mouth watered as he saw that his huge plate of grilled cheese sandwiches was ready — with a cheery red blob of ketchup on each one!

Nice one, Zepp, he thought. He'd missed ketchup badly out here in space.

Kaal made a face as he sat down. "I know your Earth food is weird, but that is something else!"

"Try one!" John said, cramming a grilled cheese into his mouth and chewing. "You might like them."

"Animal juices curdled into a paste, then melted over half-scorched slabs of plant mush?" Kaal looked ill.

"We really should try it," Emmie said. "Come on, Kaal. How many times has John tried our food on this ship? It's our turn."

"Okay," said Kaal. "You go first, though."

"Oh well," Emmie said. "Here goes." She took a deep breath, then nibbled a tiny bit off the edge of one of the little sandwiches.

Then she took a bigger bite, and smiled at John. "It's delicious!"

"Told you," John said.

"It's amazing!" Emmie said. "Tastes like . . . I dunno . . . like being cozy and warm under the Sillaran sun."

Kaal picked up a sandwich by the corner and dangled it as if it were a horrible-smelling sock. He gave John a wary, nervous look and then took a bite. His face told John exactly what he thought.

"Sorry," John said with a grin. Emmie shrugged and helped herself to another sandwich.

Kaal swallowed as if he were forcing down a golf ball. "Zepp, get me a Gyronic surprise, quick," he said. "I need to get the taste out of my mouth. . . ."

The Gyronic surprise looked like a bowl of rainwater that rats had drowned in. A strange rainbow-colored scum drifted over the top of it. Unidentifiable lumpy masses stirred in the thick morass beneath. Kaal quickly lifted the bowl to his mouth with both hands and drank from it deeply.

"I'm heading back to the lab," John announced, pushing his empty plate away.

Good thing I finished those sandwiches before Kaal started slurping that stuff, he thought. *He'd have made me lose my appetite!*

"I'm heading back to the lab too!" Emmie said. "I've got some tweaking to do. I can't seem to get Cammy to go into fight mode. She prefers hiding."

"I'll be in the dorm," Kaal said, wiping his mouth. "I've already finished Laserdon, so I think I might video call my family."

"Laserdon?" John raised an eyebrow. "Why's your robot called that?"

"You'll see why soon enough!" Kaal said mysteriously.

As John watched Kaal jump up from the table, he hid his disappointment. He'd hoped that if Kaal had finished his own robot, he might offer to help John complete his. After all, wasn't that the kind of thing a best friend would usually do?

But then John caught himself; he was determined to do this by himself anyway, wasn't he? He would have probably turned down such an offer, but he was still surprised.

* * *

Back in the lab, John worked like he'd never worked before. The console ate up his raw materials and ejected custom-made components. They only took seconds to make, but it was still frustrating to even have to wait that long.

John fitted each new piece into place as soon it was delivered, feeding fresh scrap materials into a hopper on the side.

Attach the leg servos, then screw the neck in place, then bolt the head on, then clamp the ear antennae onto the sides . . .

Super-Rover was looking a lot more like a dog now, but the clock on the desk-com was already reading 7:46 p.m., and he didn't even have his weapons yet. Sitting up and barking wouldn't be much use against the likes of IFI . . . or any other robot, if it came to that.

At least John had Super-Rover's remote control handset ready. It was held together with molecular binding strips, but he was pretty sure it would work.

Across the lab, Emmie was making frantic adjustments to Cammy's electronic brain. The hovering skimmer's cockpit was open, and its skin was pulsing with patterns that didn't match the surroundings at all, but were still beautiful — rolling open skies, strange red-orange rocky landscapes: a digital waltz of computer-generated forms.

John had never seen a more stunning robot. Even if Emmie struggled with the technical side of things, she definitely had a talent for art and design.

His own Super-Rover looked kind of lame next to Cammy, like a mutt made of old tin cans. But John knew there was a lot of power under that metallic skin. He'd plugged it in there himself. Now if only the components would hurry up. . . .

The clock now read 7:54 p.m. Super-Rover's freshly made, razor-sharp tail clonked into the delivery tray. Working quickly, but careful not to cut himself, John wrestled it into place.

Now Super-Rover only needed his teeth. John had sliced the old beronzium claw into bits with a high-beam laser cutter earlier, and now he tipped everything into the hopper. As he waited for the teeth to arrive, he heard an ominous low hum. An Examiner came drifting into the room.

The sound always made John's hair stand on end, thinking of the first time he had met them.

It must be coming to collect the robots! John realized. He glanced around and saw that everyone else was finished. He was the last.

"Come on!" he whispered to the console. Nothing happened.

In a moment of frustration, he thumped it. Suddenly, like a slot machine paying out, the console dropped freshly made metal dog's teeth into the tray. Finally!

"You have one minute to finish assembling

your robots," the Examiner intoned. "Countdown begins."

It's okay. I can do this. Piece of cake.

John began to fit the teeth into the sockets already set in Super-Rover's jaw. The first clicked home. The second, he fumbled. It went spinning across the floor.

"Fifty seconds."

John dived after it and managed to snatch it up. "Ouch. That's sharp!"

"Forty seconds."

He clicked it into place and grabbed for the rest. The tray came off in his hand, sending loose teeth rattling everywhere like puzzle pieces. John groaned in dismay.

"Thirty seconds."

"Come on!" John told himself desperately, as he picked up the teeth and tried to cram them into place. "Don't mess it up now!"

"Twenty seconds."

I'm not going to make it, he thought.

"Ten, nine, eight . . ."

Gaaah! Why did I design this?

John was sweating as he clicked the last row of teeth into place. His hair had fallen into his face, but he didn't even have time to brush it away.

All done. But wait — no, there was a gap. A tooth was missing.

"Four, three, two . . ."

There it was on the floor, almost under the console. He grabbed it and shoved it in. Sharp metal dug into his finger, drawing blood.

"Ow!"

". . . One. *Bzzzzt.* Time is now up. Step away from your robots. If you do not step away from your robots, they will be destroyed."

John moved away from Super-Rover, sucking

on his injured finger. "That was too close," he said.

The Examiner came drifting over. A single glowing eye wafted back and forth across its digital faceplate.

It angled its head toward Super-Rover, and a blast of red light engulfed the little robot. Then it was completely gone.

CHAPTER 5

The Examiner moved on across the classroom. John felt as if the floor had fallen out from under him.

"They destroyed him!" he blurted. "They destroyed Super-Rover! That's not fair. I finished in time! I know I did!"

"John, John, it's okay!" Emmie insisted. "The Examiner's just teleporting the robots for safekeeping overnight!"

John looked again.

He could see all the robots were being

zapped away. Cammy vanished in a red flash as he watched.

"Oh," he said. "Phew. Sorry. I'm a little excited. Sorry."

"Come on. Let's get some rest," Emmie said with a grin. "After all, you don't want to be all sleepy when the competition starts tomorrow, do you?"

"I don't know if I can sleep now," John said. "It's too exciting."

"Looking forward to it now?" Emmie asked with a smile.

"You know what? I think I am."

Especially if Super-Rover gets to crunch that robot of Mordant Talliver's like a dog with a bone . . .

* * *

John slept uneasily that night.

He dreamed that a crowd of Examiners was chasing him down a never-ending hallway, firing beams of red light at him.

When his alarm went off, he sat bolt upright, breathing hard.

"Quick, get dressed, John!" Kaal called from his side of the dorm. "The competition starts in twenty minutes, and we definitely don't want to be late."

John pulled on his clothes, feeling nervous and apprehensive. All the excitement of the day before seemed to have evaporated overnight. Now he just felt like he was going to be tested and, in all likelihood, fall at the first hurdle.

There were hundreds of students at the school, most of them older and more experienced than he was, and there were only going to be six finalists.

He'd never made a robot before. Why was

he even trying to compete, with the odds stacked against him like that? They must be thousands to one.

And what if he looked like a joke in front of the whole school?

I have to make it through to the final somehow, he decided. *I've got just as much of a right to be there as any of them. I belong here.*

"Wake up time!" Zepp said, and a full glass emerged slowly through the top of the bedside table.

John rubbed sleep out of his eyes and tried to focus. "Is that orange juice?"

"It's orange, and it's juice . . . that's what you wanted, right?"

John sipped it and made a face. "This tastes like bat poop!"

"Lots of things in the universe have orange-colored juice," said Zepp, sounding confused.

"Anyhow, you need to be at the Sonic Sports Hall in ten minutes."

"Where's that?" John asked.

"Come on," Kaal said impatiently. "If you're quick, I'll show you."

John drank down the glass of juice that was orange in color but had nothing to do with oranges and headed out of the room.

John wondered if the Sonic Sports Hall was on some deep level of the ship he'd never been to yet. Hyperspace High was full of unexplored corridors and shifting walkways. But Kaal seemed to be leading him to the normal gyms on the other side of the ship. John didn't think any of them could possibly be big enough for the competition.

When they reached the large, brilliantly lit gymnasium, he understood. The dividing walls between all the gyms had sunk into the floor —

he could see the faint lines where they had been — and this created one enormous wide-open space.

"The teachers can remodel the ship," Kaal explained. "It can even split into separate ships in an emergency."

"Cool," John said, impressed. But his mind was saying something else: *How can I ever learn my way around in this school if the walls don't even stay in one place?*

The Sonic Sports Hall was big enough to dock an aircraft carrier. From the ceiling hung racks of spotlights and force-field generators, able to suspend students in bubbles of elastic energy for games of Zero-G Impactball or to create instant arenas for martial arts duels. Matter stream cylinders could provide any surface needed for sports — sand, earth, water, and even lava — and disintegrate it again afterward.

The robots were stationed at the near end of the hall, arranged in a neat row, and in faintly glowing starting zones. Two Examiners hovered over them, keeping a careful watch.

John saw Electric E, IFI, Quondass's huge drill-like robot, one that looked like a trash can with short, dumpy legs, and several others — more than he had time to count.

And there was Super-Rover, sitting on his haunches like a real dog, as if he were waiting patiently for John.

At the far end of the hall was a faint blue light, filling the space from the floor to the ceiling.

A section of floor had been raised to make a stage. Master Tronic stood there, just visible behind the crowd of students that had already begun to gather.

"Welcome to the contest!" he boomed. "The

first round is a simple test of speed. The first six robots to cross the finish line in each year group will be the winners of this very first round!" He gestured with a metal fist to the glimmering blue field.

"Sounds simple enough," Kaal said, shrugging.

"Yeah," said John. "It's not rocket science, is it?"

Kaal looked puzzled. "Of course not," he answered. "This is Robotics. Rocket Science is next term."

John rolled his eyes and went to join the crowd that was already checking out the robots. With more than a thousand robots to see, it was like being at some kind of futuristic art exhibition.

Some of the older students had done unbelievable work. A crowd had gathered around Prince Karfelan, a tall, grey-skinned alien with oval black eyes, who had built a robot that was a living swarm of tiny, smaller robots. *Stylish,* John thought, *but not as fast as his own little dog robot.*

John turned his attention to the competition from his own year. Many were obviously no-hopers — jumbled, botched, or just plain weird, like the centipede with an air horn for a nose or the thing like a goldfish bowl on triangular wheels. Maybe John had a better chance than he thought!

"Competitors!" roared Master Tronic. "Take your places behind your robots! If you have controllers, activate them now!"

With his heart beating madly, John went and stood behind Super-Rover and switched on his controller.

To his right, Kaal was firing up a controller

of his own. His robot, Laserdon, was hawk-like, with a fierce light burning in its eyes.

"I reckon you're in with a good chance in this round," John told him. "Laserdon looks *fast*!"

"Not as fast as Cammy," Kaal said modestly, looking over at Emmie's sleek robot. "Have you seen Silverfire, though? Shazilda's built her for nothing *but* speed!"

Shazilda was a cocky, purple-skinned girl from the planet Pellgrayne; her robot looked like a rotating silver bullet, hovering a few inches above the ground.

"The race will begin in ten seconds!" Master Tronic announced, the red light in his head now pulsing furiously.

"Good luck," John said to Kaal. His friend returned a determined smile.

A high-pitched whistle sounded.

In the next second, the hall was filled with the whirring, buzzing, thrumming, screeching noises of a thousand robots launching themselves into the race.

Aluminum-covered cockroaches raced against trundling battle tanks. Scuttling pyramids with wobbly eyes shouldered aside chattering androids with chomping jaws.

But out in front of all of them was Silverfire, rushing through the air like a high-tech express train.

Super-Rover was hot on Silverfire's trail. John rammed his speed control up to full, steering him around other robots that had capsized, suffered power failure, or — in one case — burst into flames.

Super-Rover's springy little legs were a blur. John bashed the jump button, sending Super-Rover in a graceful leap over a burning robot.

Laserdon glided along behind them. Kaal's face was a green mask of pure concentration.

Silverfire whizzed into the blue field, finishing first out of the whole contest, followed closely by Dol's eel-like robot.

There was nobody else in front. John leaned into the final stretch, sure of finishing next. But then Cammy appeared out of nowhere, right ahead of him!

He heard Emmie laugh.

"Surprise!" she said, as her streamlined camouflage robot whizzed through the blue field.

Super-Rover charged through the field seconds later.

John leaped up and punched the air. He'd done it — the first round was down!

Laserdon was hot on Super-Rover's heels, and John saw Kaal smiling at his achievement.

John quickly counted — only one more place left.

The remaining robots wheezed and whined as they struggled to cross the distance. IFI zipped in front of them, moving easily on its force field. As John looked on, Mordant's robot swerved out in front of two others, a barrel-like stomper and an elegant tripod.

The barrel swerved, too, trying to avoid IFI, and smashed into the tripod, sending it toppling over. The students controlling them yelled angrily.

"Cunning move, sir!" said G-Vez. "Nothing in the rules that says you can't go sideways, is there, sir?"

"That's two less losers to worry about," gloated Mordant. "Okay, I'm bored now. Let's go." He pressed a control, and IFI zoomed silently over the finish line.

"And he is through to the next round!" G-Vez cheered.

"I could have been first if I'd wanted to," Mordant said. He put his hands behind his head as if this had all been too easy.

"Of course!" G-Vez said.

"The race is now over!" announced Master Tronic as the field suddenly turned red with a buzz.

There was a chorus of disappointed *awwww* sounds from the gathered students. The hall was still full of robots ponderously tromping toward the finish. John felt a little sorry for them, despite his own victory.

"All those who have qualified for the next round will now be transferred to the ship's main hangar," Master Tronic said. "To save time, we will be using sonic transference!"

John had only a second to wonder what that

was. Then a dizzy feeling came over him, and his vision started to blur. . . .

CHAPTER 6

The next thing John knew, he was standing in the hangar. It was a huge space, easily as big as the Sonic Sports Hall, with one of the room's sides closed off by a gigantic set of vertical sliding doors.

Beyond those doors lay nothing but space itself. It always gave John an uneasy feeling to think about how close that never-ending void really was.

The sonic transference waves had set down the students in order of year. John found he was standing with Shazilda, Emmie, Kaal, Mordant, and Dol the P'Sidion.

"I guess we're through to round two!" Emmie said, smiling.

"Give that girl a gold star," Mordant scoffed. He rolled his eyes and added, "Of course we are, you moron. Why else would we all be standing here?"

Before John could say what he was thinking, Master Tronic began his next announcement.

"This is the Black Tunnel Test!" Master Tronic said. "In this round, we will test your robots' agility. Speed and weapons count for nothing. Only careful maneuvering will see you through."

Master Tronic pressed a button on his arm. Suddenly, a swirling black opening like an upright whirlpool appeared in front of the contestants. It formed one end of a long, flat-bottomed tube that extended away from Master Tronic's podium and wound around the hangar in a zigzagging, spiraling maze, returning in a circle to open back out at the podium.

"This'll be easy," Mordant snorted. "Even with all those twists, the tunnel's three times as wide as any robot here."

"I should probably mention," Master Tronic added with a hint of menace, "that the tunnel is self-adjusting. It will shrink to fit whichever robot enters it. You will have very little clearance to work with."

"Shows *you*, Mordant," bubbled Dol.

Master Tronic continued. "Rules of this round are simple. The aim is to guide your robot through the black tunnel without touching the sides or the top. You may, of course, touch the floor."

It's like those buzz games, John thought. *With*

the wiggly metal wire and the loop you have to weave around it. I was always pretty good at those!

To his surprise, some of the older students were whispering among themselves. John saw nervous faces.

"What's up with them?" he asked Kaal. "Are they worried about this or something?"

"None of them were prepared for anything like this," Kaal said. "This challenge has never been in the contest before."

"Good!" Emmie said. "That means we're all equal."

Mordant Talliver rolled his eyes. "As if," he said.

Dol raised her flipper-like arm. "Sir? Is there a time limit?"

"Good question," the robot-bodied teacher said. "You have fifteen minutes each to complete the test, but most students do not take that long."

Surprised murmurs broke out among the students.

"Like I said, speed is not the point of this round," Master Tronic repeated firmly. "However, if your robot so much as brushes the sides or top of the tunnel, you are out of the competition. Any other questions?"

"How are we supposed to see our robots inside that tunnel?" asked Kaal hesitantly. "To guide them, I mean."

Master Tronic held up a pair of goggles. "We've thought of that," he said. "These special goggles will let you see through the tunnel walls. Everyone else can watch the robots go through the tunnel on the tracker-cam, since a plain black tunnel isn't all that interesting to look at." He pointed to a huge screen on the wall and then said, "Now, would anyone care to volunteer to go first?"

John heard Emmie take a deep breath. "I'll go," she said. Then she turned to John and whispered, "May as well get this over and done with."

"Good luck, Emmie," John said, patting her on the shoulder. He crossed his fingers. "You'll do great."

Behind him, Mordant was talking to G-Vez. "Get IFI ready for me, would you? That hopeless piece of trash is going to screw up at the first bend."

G-Vez made a noise that sounded like a laugh, and asked, "Are you referring to Miss Tarz, or to her unfortunate robot?"

"Take your pick," Mordant said with a shrug. "Though since you mentioned it, the robot's probably brighter than she is. And I heard she borrowed its brain from a broken-down toilet-cleaner droid."

Emmie's face showed no sign that she'd heard a thing. She pulled on the goggles, then used her remote control to steer Cammy to the opening.

"Whenever you're ready," Master Tronic said. "Take your time."

Cammy slowly moved through the opening and into the tunnel. To John's horror, the robot's skin immediately shifted to a deep black.

"Oh no, Cammy, not now!" Emmie said despairingly. Mordant burst out laughing. Emmie fiddled with the controls, but Cammy remained almost invisible against the black tunnel wall.

John crossed his fingers even tighter. But it did no good.

John watched the tracker-cam screen, which showed a view of Cammy from behind. Emmie was struggling to move her robot around even the gentle starting bends. It was just too hard to see where she was.

"Only one working feature on that stupid robot, and it's making it harder for her," Mordant said, laughing meanly. "Wow, Emmie must be some kind of genius."

Emmie tried to steer Cammy around a U-bend turn. Instantly, a warning siren blared. One of Cammy's tail fins was sticking through the wall.

"Oh, shooting stars!" Emmie said disgustedly, throwing up her hands.

The tunnel dissolved into a flurry of black pixels. Cammy appeared at Emmie's feet.

"Sorry, Emmie," John said. He felt sorry for Emmie, but he was also a little bit relieved. At least Emmie's humiliation was over quickly. It hadn't lasted long.

"Oh, it's okay," she said, with a big smile

that John didn't really believe. "It's only a game, isn't it? Just having fun. It's not about winning — not really."

But her knuckles were still white where she had gripped the remote control, and with her other hand she was bending the antenna as if she wanted to break it.

"I'll go next," Mordant said, pushing to the front. "Watch and learn."

A new version of the twisting tunnel appeared, resized to fit IFI. Mordant pulled the goggles on without waiting for permission and sent IFI humming into the tunnel mouth.

John watched the cone-shaped robot on the tracker-cam. It was zooming through the tunnel almost as quickly as it had raced through the Sonic Sports Hall. Mordant took even the tightest corners at high speed, without so much as breaking a sweat.

Something about his self-assured arrogance made John wonder. He thought back to how G-Vez had bounced off IFI's protective force field. Was it even *possible* for Mordant's robot to touch the walls with that force field surrounding it?

After only a few minutes, IFI emerged through the other end of the tunnel. "Yes!" Mordant yelled. "That's how it's done. Smooth as silk!"

There was an awkward silence. Mordant looked around, obviously waiting for applause.

"Amazing performance, sir!" G-Vez crooned. "No one will be able to beat that. The prize is as good as yours!"

"Who's the robot master?" Mordant shouted, hopping up and down on the spot in an absurd little victory dance. "I *said*, who's the robot master?"

John wondered if Mordant had any idea how ridiculous he looked. Not one single student said a word to him.

John was glad he hadn't rushed to go first. He was getting a little familiar with the tunnel, just by watching the other two go through it on the tracker-cam.

The real killer was the U-bend about halfway through. He'd have to be extra careful when Super-Rover reached it.

Some older students had their turns, and then Kaal was up. Like John, he'd been studying the tunnel carefully.

As Kaal activated Laserdon and sent him flapping into the air, John felt anxious on his behalf. It would be very tricky to keep a flying robot from bumping into the ceiling. It was funny how what helped you in one round could work against you in the next.

That must be the point, John thought. *The winning robot would have to be an all-star.*

"Here we go," Kaal said nervously.

Laserdon flew into the whirling tunnel like a hawk plunging into the mouth of a cave.

At least Kaal knows what it's like to fly. He has wings of his own. That's got to help, doesn't it?

Kaal flew his robot cautiously, negotiating the tangled tunnel foot by foot. He was past the deadly U-bend now and heading down the slope toward the exit.

Just then, Mordant coughed loudly.

John saw Kaal frown, distracted by the noise. It was only a split-second distraction, but it was enough. Laserdon was still flying level — and the tunnel was about to slope down.

John held his breath.

Kaal quickly nudged the controls. Laserdon swooped down, avoiding the sloping ceiling by half an inch. The robot flew gracefully down the exit tunnel and slid straight back out into the hangar.

Kaal held out his arm and Laserdon landed on it, clamping on with robotic claws. Kaal was smiling in sheer delight. John gave him a thumbs-up.

A rubbery tentacle nudged John in the back. "You're up next, human. Man, I really wish I'd thought to bring something to read. I just have this feeling that you're going to take *hours* to get your robot through that tunnel."

All eyes were on John.

He sent Super-Rover trotting to the mouth of the black tunnel. He felt the pressure of thousands of eyes watching him. It had gotten quiet in the hangar — so quiet, John could hear the faint echo of his own footsteps.

He pulled on the goggles, and the tunnel

seemed to become smoky and transparent. He could see through it to where the little robotic dog sat, waiting faithfully for his owner's instructions.

"Whenever you're ready," Master Tronic said.

A wave of nervousness washed over John as he thought of the whole school watching.

I can do this, he told himself. *I'm good at those buzzer games. Excellent spatial awareness, my dad always says. He says I'll make a good driver once I'm old enough.*

He moved the controls, and Super-Rover walked into the tunnel. Slowly, cautiously, he guided the little robot around the first long bend, keeping him clear of the sides.

Then there was an upward spiral, followed by a zigzag. He fought against the urge to speed up.

It doesn't matter if I take hours. I can't hurry this. That's what Mordant wants.

Super-Rover trotted down a short slope, his antenna ears almost brushing the ceiling.

Easy does it, John told himself. *Okay! Great! We made it!*

Now there was a long curve back the other way, so he could relax a little.

It's not so different from flying my little remote control helicopter back on Earth, he realized. *Okay, so it's a robotic dog. And this is outer space. And a bunch of aliens are staring at me. But* apart *from that, it's not so different.*

Now he had to contend with that dreaded U-bend, the most dangerous spot in the whole test. Already it had finished more robots than any other section.

John slowed Super-Rover down to a slow crawl. The robot paced carefully around the bend, a few inches at a time. Any slower, and he would have fallen over sideways.

Just then, John heard Mordant give a loud, sarcastic yawn.

He gritted his teeth. *Yawn all you want, Talliver. I'm not speeding up.*

But the hard work of concentrating was beginning to wear on John. He was sweating all over, and his hands felt clammy.

Super-Rover plodded out of the bend. Excitement took hold of John. The worst part was behind him now. After all the drama of the day before, he was in, with a real chance of making it to the final!

He guided Super-Rover around another, gentler bend, up a rise, and through the last zigzag.

Almost at the end now.

John was trembling all over, though whether

that was from nerves or excitement he didn't know. No doubt it was some of both.

Everyone watched as Super-Rover came trotting down the last slope.

I might just do it, John realized, the final in his sights. *I'm nearly there.*

But the more he fought not to screw up, the more certain he became that he would do something awful.

Keep calm, he told himself. *Be cool, John.*

But his hands were shaking as if he'd had a nasty shock. The remote control suddenly felt slippery in his hands. He tightened his grip, afraid to drop it. There was a faint click as his thumb accidentally pressed a button.

Super-Rover's tail began to wag slowly, whipping back and forth in the tight tunnel.

"Oh no," John said, horrified. "No, stop that! Stop! Bad dog!"

Super-Rover just wagged his tail more, as if delighted to see John again.

Mordant sniggered and said, "Oh, what a shame. You were so close."

Super-Rover was only a few feet from the exit now. But his tail was thrashing faster and faster, coming closer and closer to the tunnel's sides. . . .

If that tail even so much as grazes the side, I'm out of the contest! John thought, fighting to get Super-Rover back under control.

The controller felt as cumbersome as a lead weight in his hands. He thumbed the tail control, but the tail just wouldn't stop wagging.

There must be a short circuit, John thought in desperation. The tail wagged faster and faster. Any second now and it would swish into the tunnel wall.

There was only one way to get Super-

Rover out of there before that happened. In desperation, John hit the rocket booster.

CHAPTER 7

Super-Rover shot out of the tunnel like a cannonball and tumbled head over heels across the hangar floor. He came to rest at John's feet, sat on his haunches, and looked up. His tail still wagged madly.

"Good boy," John said, too amazed to think straight.

No siren. No buzz. The tunnel hadn't vanished. *Does that mean . . .*

"Congratulations, John Riley," boomed Master Tronic. "You are through to the next round. A pity there are no bonus points for a dramatic finish."

Instantly, Kaal and Emmie were at John's side.

"You did it!" Emmie said, slapping him on the back. "That was fantastic!"

Relief flooded over John. He looked down at his hands, which were still shaking.

"Are you *sure* you've never done this before?" Kaal asked suspiciously.

"First time. Honest!" John noticed that the grin on Kaal's face was wavering. His friend didn't see him as competition, did he? But then Kaal held up his hand for a high five, and John, feeling silly for worrying, smacked his palm. Emmie did the same.

"Why are you hitting each other?" Dol asked, her beady little eyes wide with horror.

"It's an Earth victory custom," Emmie

explained. "When your friends score an 'epic win,' you bash hands together. It's fun."

Dol bubbled with laughter and slapped her own flipper against Emmie's outstretched hand. "My people usually just whistle," she said modestly.

John smiled to see Emmie happy again. She looked like she'd forgotten all about her own failure and instead just wanted to congratulate John and Kaal. Warmth seemed to shine from her.

His victory was starting to sink in. He'd done it. He'd really done it.

Right now, John thought, *I wouldn't change places with anyone in the universe.* This was a perfect moment, and nothing could ruin it.

Behind him, he could hear other students cheering and congratulating one another. Without thinking, he turned around to join in.

"High five!" he yelled, slapping the tentacle that came up to meet his. "It's an, uh, Earth victory . . . custom. . . ."

Mordant Talliver was standing there, smirking. "That's really sporting of you, Earth boy," he said. "Nice of you to recognize your betters. So that's a high five, is it?"

"So-called because Earthlings have five digits on each hand," G-Vez butted in.

"How quaint. Maybe you can give me another of those high fives when I win the contest."

Not if I can help it, you slippery half-Gargon jerk, John thought.

* * *

"Victory feast!" John said, sitting down in the Center.

The table was spread with food, organized into three neat sections. His own had a stack of cheese toasties, a huge bowl of corn chips, some bowls of what he hoped were dip, and some crusty sausage rolls.

"A little early for that, isn't it?" Kaal said. "I know we've both done well so far, but still . . ."

"Victory lunch break, then," Emmie said, digging in. "Gotta say, though. If you two keep this up, I won't know who to cheer for! After all, you can't *both* win."

They all laughed.

"What *is* that stuff?" John had to ask, pointing at Kaal's own collection of little bowls. They looked worryingly similar to John's own dips, and he didn't want to mix them up.

"Acheron wasp eggs, mashed scab-root, and Jengeroon spit. Want some?"

John silently moved his bowls of dip farther

away from Kaal's. "Um, no thanks," he said. "I'll pass."

The next round was back in the main auditorium. This time, John made sure the three of them went in together, with plenty of time to spare. He sat between Kaal and Emmie in one of the center rows.

Up on the stage stood the ten robots that had made it through the Black Tunnel Test. They looked very small next to the three grim-looking, unknown machines that stood nearby.

Despite their futuristic casings and blinking lights, the machines looked somewhat familiar. One had huge, crushing, vice-like arms, another dangled a flat weight from a glowing green force-cable above an X mark, and yet another had a track leading up to a wide flat wall.

Even more alarming were the three Examiners who hovered nearby, holding strange devices in their manipulation fields that looked like laptops with egg whisks welded on.

"What are those things?" John wondered aloud. "And why do you think we're up here instead of down there?"

"Well, they haven't given us our controllers back," Kaal mused. "So I guess they want to see how well our robots do on their own."

"I don't get it," Emmie frowned. "What can a robot do without an operator?"

John felt uneasy looking at the big machines. Where had he seen them before? Something he'd watched with his dad . . .

Then it came to him: *Top Gear.* These machines looked like car-crash testers.

"Oh no," he said. "Guys . . ."

"Waaaait," Emmie said. "I get it! They're going to smash them up, aren't they?"

Before John could say anything else, Master

Tronic stepped onto the podium. "Welcome to Round Three! As you can see, the Examiners have been kind enough to assist me with the judging for this one."

A tense silence hung over the hall. Nobody was ever glad to see an Examiner.

"This round measures robot strength and durability," Master Tronic continued. "Each robot will be put through its paces in a series of punishing tests. Six lucky robots out of these ten will make it through to the semi-finals. The remaining four —" and here his metal skull throbbed ominously — "will not be so lucky."

"Those are pretty good odds," Kaal whispered to John. "Better than fifty percent . . ." But in spite of his words, he was rubbing his hands together nervously.

John could guess why. Kaal had needed to make Laserdon quite lightweight, to allow him to fly. And only the most robust robots would survive this round, that was certain.

"And the first robot to be tested, determined by random chance, is . . ."

John held his breath.

"Super-Rover, built by John Riley, from Earth!"

"Oh, great," said John, burying his face in his palm. "I don't know if I can watch this." He felt Emmie squeeze his shoulder.

An Examiner picked up Super-Rover in its manipulation field, placed him carefully between the two vice-like crushers, and backed away. The little robot's tail was still wagging from the last round, unable to stop. Somehow, that made this even worse.

"Begin!" Master Tronic declared sternly.

The arms of the vice closed. John didn't want to watch, but he couldn't make himself look away. There was a long, drawn-out *crrrrrunk* as Super-Rover was squeezed. A high-pitched electronic sound came from somewhere inside him.

It's just his servos adjusting, John thought.

But it had sounded exactly like a sad little puppy whine.

After far too long, the arms of the vice separated. John watched gloomily, expecting his robot to topple over like a piece of scrap. But although his tail was wagging much more slowly and one of his ears was bent, Super-Rover was still working!

"Go on, Super-Rover!" Emmie yelled suddenly. "You can take it!"

The watching students burst out laughing. A few of them even clapped and cheered.

Unfortunately for Super-Rover, the tests were far from finished. The Examiner placed him on an X mark beneath a flat-bottomed metal weight.

John winced. He knew exactly what was going to happen next. And sure enough, there followed a loud *CLANNNNGGGGG*.

The Examiners looked at the readouts on the machine and made notes. Master Tronic nodded to them.

The weight reeled back up. Super-Rover was splayed beneath, his four legs sticking out like the X he was lying on.

John crossed his fingers and hoped as hard as he could.

With a grinding *sproinging* sound like a broken clock, Super-Rover staggered to his feet. He didn't look good. There were a few whoops, yells, and gurgles from the audience.

"Come on, little guy," John muttered. "Hang in there . . . it's almost over now."

"John, it can't actually feel anything," Emmie said, a look of deep concern on her face. "It's just a robot. Did you think —"

"I know!" he interrupted. "I just don't understand why they're doing this. All the robots are going to be busted up before the semi-final!"

"I think we'll get a chance to fix them," Kaal said, but he didn't sound too sure. "So long as they aren't too badly damaged, they should be fine."

John looked back at the stage, just in time to see the Examiner putting Super-Rover into a wire cradle on the third machine, the one with the long rail and the wall at the end. It stood back, and its light changed from red to green.

Super-Rover whizzed down the rail in a blur of blinding speed and slammed head-first into the wall.

This time he did fall over, making a sound

exactly like John's father putting the cans out for recycling. *Crash.*

Oh well, John thought miserably. *I tried.*

But then, to John's total surprise, Super-Rover struggled to his feet again. Bent and crippled, he started to waddle towards the front of the stage, little blue sparks pinging off him as he went.

As the audience broke into spontaneous cheering, the Examiners rushed after him.

"He made it!" Emmie said happily. "He survived!"

"Looks like his steering controls broke, though," Kaal said. "He was going the wrong way there. That test was rough."

But John was smiling. "They didn't break," he said. "I gave him a homing system! He knew he needed to be fixed, so he was trying to go home."

"*Home?*" Emmie asked, confused.

"To the technology lab, where he was made. It's the closest thing to a home he's got."

John could relax a little now that Super-Rover had survived his ordeal. There was no way to know whether he'd made it to the next round, but at least he hadn't been squashed flat or smashed to bits.

John sat and watched the rest of the robots being crushed, dented, flattened, pummeled, and slammed around.

Laserdon was the last to go, Kaal covering his face with his enormous hands throughout his robot's entire ordeal, until at last Master Tronic took to the podium again. He had a ThinScreen in one of his metal hands, covered with information.

A hush fell over the whole auditorium. Spellbound, the audience waited for the results.

But Master Tronic said nothing.

Suddenly, just as the students were beginning to murmur, all the lights went dim.

Master Tronic turned his head to look up, his red eyes glowing into the blackness.

There followed a sound of churning machinery. From the darkness high overhead, a great gleaming claw descended from a bundle of metal cables. It whirred back and forth above the students, as if a titanic robotic beast lurking above were searching for something.

"It's time to pick out the winners!" rumbled Master Tronic.

Each student who passed the last round looked up, including John. He could see everyone's hopeful faces, willing the crane to come down and grab them.

This must be what the teddy bears in those claw games at the arcade feel like, John thought. *Waiting for the claw to move, hoping it'll stop above you. I was always bad at those. Dad said they were a waste of money. . . .*

The claw opened wide, swung — and dropped.

It came back up holding Mordant Talliver.

"Now there's a surprise," Kaal said bitterly.

Mordant beamed triumphantly as the crane hoisted him above the seats. He swung back and forth in the claw, waving at the students beneath. There were more than a few groans, and someone sarcastically muttered, "Be a shame if it dropped him, wouldn't it . . . ?"

The claw set Mordant down on the stage next to IFI. Mordant strutted back and forth, making gestures to the audience. No one clapped.

Master Tronic coughed to get Mordant's attention and shook one of his rubbery black tentacles. "Well done," he said stiffly.

The claw was on the move again. It scanned back and forth, froze, and fell — to close around the troll-like body of Quondass val Haq. Wheezing under the strain, it hauled him up and set him down beside Rocky, his track-mounted drill robot.

"I knew he'd make it through," whispered Kaal. "When Rocky went in, I thought the vice would be the one to break! Do you think he might be the Robot Warriors champion two years running?"

John sat still, almost too excited to breathe, as the claw swung over his head. But then it moved on, plucking a different student out of the crowd. She had stark white skin and six dark eyes clustered on her face, and she squealed as it lifted her up.

That's Raytanna, John thought. *Always studying. No wonder she built something so complicated.* Her robot, Charly, was like a shimmering jellyfish. It hovered in the air, metallic tentacles dangling below, a transparent casing above. You could see into the robot's electronic innards.

Every student in the room was watching the crane. John couldn't think of a more dramatic way of bringing the winners onto the stage. No matter the student's size and shape, the robotic claw could adapt.

The claw was at the other side of the hall when it picked up winner number four, a tiny alien less than half John's height, who Emmie said was called Gredilah.

"She's a third year," Emmie said. "I heard she was a semi-finalist last year, too."

"She looks like a squirrel," John said to himself. It was a wonder she could see out of all that spiky fur.

But as she swung over his head on her way

to the stage, John saw that her fur wasn't fur at all; it was a coat of rubbery spikes.

He quickly looked up at Gredilah's robot, Fop. It looked suspiciously like a life-size toy robot from Earth — an old-fashioned one, with bright eyes and doors in its chest that opened to reveal transparent cannons. It made John wonder if Gredilah's planet had been scanning Earth's television signals.

There was a clang above John. He looked up to see the claw, wide open.

It fell — and the grabbers instantly fastened *around . . . Kaal!*

John and Emmie whooped and cheered as he went sailing across the room in the grip of the claw. Kaal looked embarrassed and a little bit awkward, like a noble flying creature trapped in a cage. The crane set him down behind Laserdon.

Just as John was beginning to worry about him, Kaal gave the audience a timid grin.

"Doesn't like the limelight, does he?" Emmie whispered, nudging John in the ribs.

"Five places have been taken!" announced Master Tronic. "Only one remains!"

John hardly dared to hope. It couldn't be him, he knew it. Super-Rover looked lost up there on his own, between a frog-hopping droid and a rubber-bodied pyramid. Both those robots had done pretty well in the last round. If only he'd put a few more strengthening struts across Super-Rover's body, but there just hadn't been time.

But the next thing John knew, the auditorium was swaying around him and his ears filled with the sound of cheering. The crane had snatched him up and was rushing him over to the stage to join the others!

The swaying made him feel a bit sick, but he didn't care. He stuck his arms out through the gaps and waved them crazily. "I did it! I DID IT! Woooohoooo!"

"Congratulations to all of you!" Master Tronic boomed above the wild applause and cheers. "Tomorrow morning, the six remaining robots will enter . . . the SEMI-FINAL!"

CHAPTER 8

By the time the next day rolled around, John still felt dizzy from his success. He had to admit, he was feeling like a king.

But what he hadn't counted on was what kings throughout the ages have had to put up with — a never-ending crowd of hangers-on, desperate for his attention, clamoring for his favor. His dorm was packed with them!

This sudden shift from school outsider to overnight wonder boy was rather difficult to cope with.

"What prize are you going to ask for?" a mushroom-covered Myconian asked eagerly, puffing smelly spores into John's face.

"Right now I'd settle for some breakfast," John muttered.

The Myconian held out a bag. "Here! I've got plenty of spicy boreworm clusters! Help yourself!"

"I . . . uh . . . can't eat those," John said. "Allergies. It's an Earth thing. Sorry."

"How about a bottle of fizzy Snurtle sweat?" asked Kritta, the insect-like girl with huge, multifaceted eyes.

"Thanks, but no thanks," John said, trying to be polite. "Um, excuse me, if I could just get through . . ."

Any other day, John would have rolled out of bed and blearily groped his way to the dorm table. Today, he couldn't even see the table.

It was hidden behind a bright holographic placard, which was being waved by a small, furry pink student.

The Holo-Placards had sprung up all over Hyperspace High; handheld, programmable electronic rods that projected 3-D signs into the air above.

"Um, excuse me, sorry," John said, squeezing past.

The pink student squeaked excitedly like a rubber dog toy. "He touched me!" the pink person squealed. "He touched me!"

The placard kept changing to a new display. Right now it read WE LOVE URTH. John thought about telling him (or her?) that it wasn't spelled like that, but shook his head. The last thing he wanted to do was to make his new fans upset.

But it wasn't the only placard in the room. A

forest of them was being brandished at his end of the dorm, with similar slogans: RILEY FOR EVER, SUPER-ROVER FOR THE WIN, and HUMANZ ROCK.

Across the room, Kaal struggled through a crowd of supporters of his own. Their placards read: KAAL SOARS ABOVE YOU, DERRILIAN POWER, and LOOK INTO THE EYE OF LASERDON. At the sides of the table, the two groups of supporters glared at one another where they met.

This is worse than the Super Bowl, John thought. *Kaal's my best friend. I hope this won't come between us. What was it Emmie said yesterday? We can't both win.*

"Kaaaaal!" yelled a burly, muscular student with a huge mouth above his single eye. He punched the air, and with his other hand waved a placard that read BIG GREEN WINNING

MACHINE and had a picture on it of Kaal looking mighty.

Other students joined in. "Kaaaaaal!" they roared.

Kaal cringed and curled his wings, using them to create a wall around himself. John tried to catch his eye, but Kaal was trying to hide from everyone — and everyone included John, it seemed.

Kaal's fans were holding out boxes of food and cups of gluey-looking drinks to him. John saw him glancing across to the shower cubicle, obviously wondering if he could get away with going for yet another shower.

He's had two already, John thought, smiling. *But it's a good idea — it's the only way to get any privacy!*

"Apple juice, please, Zepp," John said.

Everyone craned in to see what John was

having. There were some curious *oohs* and *aaahs* as his drink arrived.

John looked around, feeling overwhelmed. This was getting out of hand. Half his fans were shouting at Kaal's. The other half were trying to fetch him things. No sooner had his cup of juice arrived than someone pressed a corkscrew-like alien utensil into his hands. Someone else tried to pass him a rubbery nose-hose. Then a fork the size of a gardening trowel. He had to go and get a straw himself.

But he couldn't enjoy his juice with so many eyes watching him. And Kaal seemed really uncomfortable, too, barely touching his cup of galvanic sludge.

"Ah, he's up!" came a voice from behind John.

John turned to see a shining blue blob, moving like animated molten metal, come slurping through the door into the dorm room. It held a ThinScreen in one wavering pseudopod.

"Got plenty of rest, I hope?" the student asked.

John struggled to remember the student's name. "Yes, thanks . . . er . . ."

"Don't crowd him, Xyglurz," squeaked the little fuzzy alien. "We were here first."

"Yeah! Back off," said Kritta. "Leave this to the real fans!"

Xyglurz laughed. The sound was like a fingernail moving along a guitar string. "I was backing John before any of you!" He waved the ThinScreen. "How many of you have put together a profile on him, huh?"

Now John remembered. While he'd been repairing Super-Rover last night, Xyglurz had been firing questions at him, pestering him for information about Earth, his family, what people ate, and even what they did in the bathroom. It was all a little too personal.

This must be what star football players on Earth feel like, John thought, *when the newspaper and TV reporters wait outside their houses to hammer them with questions . . .*

"So how are you feeling about the finals today?" Xyglurz asked, ThinScreen at the ready.

John pushed away his untouched juice. "Well, it's all been pretty sudden, to be honest . . . hasn't really sunk in yet . . ."

"Listen to that," said the fuzzy pink creature. "He's a true sportsman, isn't he? A real champion. So modest."

"Not as modest as KAAAAAAL!" boomed the one-eyed giant, and they all started yelling at one another again.

Better get dressed while they're all distracted, John thought.

But it wasn't that easy. His fans insisted on bringing him his clothes, and a few of them were even trying his things on themselves. In the end, he had to pull his clothes back out of their grasp, lock himself in the bathroom alone, and get dressed there.

Alone for a few precious moments, he leaned against the wall and closed his eyes. This was *not* something he'd ever expected to have to deal with.

"Fame at last," he said to himself. "You did it, Riley. If your Earth friends could see you now!"

There must be over a hundred people cheering me on, he thought as he dressed. *They've never heard of Earth before, but they'll remember it now! In your face, Mordant Talliver!*

When he came back out, his fans all had questions ready to fire at him.

"What's Earth like?" piped the fluffy pink creature.

"Are you really descended from primates?" barked a walrus-like being.

"What gave you the idea for such an unusual robot?" asked Xyglurz.

John grinned. That was one question of the metallic alien's that he *didn't* mind answering. "It's based on a dog," he answered.

The fans chattered excitedly. "What's a *dog*?" several of them asked.

"It's a sort of pet animal," John explained. "With four legs and a tail and teeth, and it goes *woof*. And it wags its tail when it's happy."

"So it's quite small, then?" asked the furry pink thing. John really wished he knew its name. He couldn't just call it Furry Pink Thing all the time.

"Oh no," he said. "Dogs come in all shapes

and sizes. Some are little, like Chihuahuas and Jack Russells. But some are huge, like Great Danes and mastiffs."

"We've got a pet skrellick at home," said a bulbous-headed student whose body was luminous and transparent. John immediately thought he looked like a light bulb. "It's always getting into the ventilation pipes."

"Skrellicks do that," said Xyglurz knowingly. "They're trouble. Always on the move. What you want is a good faithful loffleclod."

"*Loffleclods!*" scoffed the walrus creature. "They're useless! They just sit there! Takes them half the day to crawl to the food dish, and the other half to crawl back!"

"At least you can rely on them to be there for you," said Xyglurz defensively.

"Only because it would take them a year to run away," scoffed the walrus.

"We had a loffleclod once," said the pink thing sadly. "It died. We didn't notice for three weeks."

"Give me a Kvellian razorbeast any day," put in the Myconian. "You get *respect* with one of those. They'll fight anything! Just don't ever let it see its own reflection. . . ."

John felt a sudden pang of nervousness as he realized how late it was getting and that he had to go to class. Then he remembered Emmie had told him there would be no classes today. All the students had the day off to watch the semi-finals and final.

"The Robot Warriors contest is a really, really big deal," she'd said the night before. "I'm so proud of you! Of you both, that is. Kaal too. Not just you, of course."

The whole day off, just for a contest. This IS a big deal.

All at once, John felt as if the artificial gravity had been turned up to max. Suddenly he realized just how much pressure was on him. He felt wobbly and faint.

More than a hundred students would be cheering him on today. That wasn't just an ego boost. It was a burden of responsibility.

What if he lost? What if he not only lost, but lost *massively*?

What if he'd just been lucky so far, and his luck was about to run out — with the whole school watching?

His mind raced.

He wasn't a genius.

He wasn't even above average.

Okay, so he'd always been good at math, but apart from that . . . what right did he have to even hope to win this contest?

What a weird feeling. He was looking

forward to the contest and dreading it, all at the same time.

He badly wanted to talk to Kaal. This wouldn't be so stressful for either of them if they could go through it together. But Kaal was surrounded by fans, unable to reach him. As John watched, Kaal got up and dived into the shower yet again to escape them.

That was the last straw. "Okay, all of you — OUT!" He began to shoo the crowd of startled fans out of the room. "We're glad you're supporting us, but we need some space!" Suddenly an idea flashed across his mind. "Tell you what — if you really want to help me and Kaal, why don't you go and save us some seats in the Center?"

"Come on!" yelled Kritta. "We'll grab the best seats in the entire place!" She dashed out of the room.

"The best seats are for the followers of KAAAAAL!" the one-eyed creature boomed, charging after her. Within moments, the room was empty.

John heaved a relieved sigh and tapped on the shower door. "Kaal? It's okay. You can come out now."

Kaal poked his head warily around the door. "Really?"

"Yep," John said. He grinned. Finally, a chance to talk to Kaal in private.

Just then, a light began to flash and a buzzer began to sound. The videophone!

"Your parents are calling, John!" Zepp told him. "Shall I send a busy signal?"

"No!" John said with a sigh.

As much as he wanted to speak to Kaal, John couldn't risk his parents calling the boarding school where he was supposed to be. What if they were calling about something important, and if he didn't answer, they tried the Wortham Court main line?

He grabbed the videophone camera and twisted it so that it faced into the corner of the room, then stood in front of it. He didn't even want to think about what would happen if his parents caught sight of Kaal.

Both his mom and dad appeared on the screen, waving.

"Hello, dear!" his mom said. "Your dad was upset he'd missed you the other day, so we thought we'd give you a call! It's not a bad time, is it?"

"Don't worry, won't keep you long," his dad said, smiling. "How's life at school?"

"Great!" John said. "Mom, Dad, there's something I need to tell you." He took a deep breath. "I'm a finalist in a contest!"

Both of his parents applauded. "That's wonderful news!" his mom said. "What sort of contest? School sports day?"

"Oh, stop it!" his dad said, jokingly. "I bet it's some sort of video game tournament. You know how much practice he's put in with those things."

"Nothing like that," John assured them. "It's . . . um . . . it's a science competition!"

"Fantastic! That's your lab, right?" his dad asked, peering into the screen at John's dorm. "Ooh. It's very futuristic."

John realized he'd pointed the camera at the dorm's high-tech drinks dispenser. "Oh, yeah. It's all ultra modern, and stuff. Wortham Court's got . . . um . . . millions of dollars for science. From the government."

"Great job, honey," his mother said, beaming with pride. "We're proud of you!"

"Thanks, Mom," John said.

Then his mother frowned and looked closer. "John?" she said nervously. "What in the world is that thing?"

John glanced behind him, sure they had seen Kaal.

But to his horror, Xyglurz had snuck back into the room and was taking notes on his ThinScreen — about John's parents, no doubt! The bathroom door was shut again, which explained where Kaal had vanished to.

"It's all blue and shiny!" his father said. "Is it some sort of metal?"

"Yes!" John yelled, lunging for the camera. "It's . . . uh . . . my experiment! Great talking to you. I have to go now, bye!"

Before they could ask any more awkward questions, John turned off the videophone. Thank goodness Xyglurz hadn't said anything.

A talking science experiment might have been one surprise too many. . . .

CHAPTER 9

John found his crowds of supporters in the main cafeteria. He felt like a warlord at the vanguard of an army. All this cheering, banner-waving, and back-slapping — a guy could get used to this!

"Got a chair for you here, John!" shouted Light Bulb (whose name, it seemed, was Fluoron). "Come on through!"

The rest of the cafeteria was already crowded with other students, but instead of the usual neat rows, they were clustered into five huge groups.

Tables and chairs had been dragged over so that the groups could sit together. It was like a battlefield, flags and pennants waving, each group crowding around its commander.

Between the groups threaded a few undecided students who hadn't yet picked a champion, and the very unfortunate few who were too behind on their studies to join in the fun.

Kaal had his crew, John had his crew, Quondass val Haq, Raytanna, and Gredilah had theirs.

Only Mordant Talliver sat alone, picking at his black gooey breakfast, with the ever-loyal G-Vez hovering over his shoulder.

He had packets of Yoko Beans, Astron Crunchies, and Brucko Gums spread out in front of him, which he offered to passers-by. A few students had taken the bait, but they were talking among themselves, not even bothering to wave the Mordant Talliver Holo-Placards he'd given them.

For a second, John considered feeling sorry for Mordant.

Nah.

"Hey, John!" Emmie called from the halfway point between John's group and Kaal's. "Good luck in the finals today!" Her Holo-Placard beamed the message GO JOHN GO.

"Thanks, Emmie. Come sit with us," John offered.

"I'm fine!" she said, glancing over her shoulder. "I'll just stand here. Don't want to get in the way . . . Hey, Kaal! Good luck!"

"Thanks, Emmie!" Kaal said with a shy wave.

John saw that the other side of Emmie's banner read GO KAAL GO. He couldn't help laughing out loud.

Emmie noticed, shrugged, and gave him a big you-got-me grin. "What can I say? I can't take sides, can I?"

"Emmie, don't ever change," John said, shaking his head in wonder.

"Okay, well, good luck to you both," Emmie said quickly. "Got to go now. I've got, um . . . things to do." With that, she was gone, bounding out of the cafeteria and leaving John puzzled.

It must be rough, not making it to the final, he thought. *Maybe Emmie couldn't put on her brave face any longer.*

The ship's nutrition system, as advised by Zepp, served John a big bowl of cornflakes. Instantly his fans crowded around him, eager to see what kinds of exotic Earth food he might be eating.

"Can I try one of those?" Xyglurz asked nervously.

"You can have the whole bowl," John said, pushing away the bowl. "To be honest, I don't have much of an appetite."

John didn't want to say it aloud, but he was feeling sick with nerves. There were only ten minutes left until the semi-final was due to start. As with all the rounds, he had no idea what to expect.

Across the table, Xyglurz was turning a strange metallic green and spitting out chunks of soggy cornflakes.

* * *

The next few minutes passed in a blur.

Before John knew it, he was standing in the main lecture hall once again, looking up at Master Tronic, who was looming above everyone's heads. All six of the finalist robots had been placed in a line at Master Tronic's feet.

The stage area had been remodeled overnight. Instead of the usual smooth, flat surface, there was a fifty-foot-wide crater of what appeared to be moon rock. It looked like a bomb had blasted it out.

Is it real, or some sort of solid hologram? John wondered. He could easily believe it had been sliced out of an actual moon with mining lasers, then hoisted aboard the ship.

"Up until now," Master Tronic was saying (with what John could have sworn was relish), "we have gone easy on the contestants."

Could have fooled me, John thought.

"Today, that will change!" Master Tronic boomed. "Welcome to the semi-finals, in which we remind ourselves why this is called the Robot WARRIORS contest!"

The crowd became a frenzy of cheers and applause. Master Tronic strode back and forth like a drill sergeant, smacking his metal fist into his hand as he spoke.

"This round is about *weapons*. This round is about *power*. This round is about *destruction*. These six robots are about to face their first real challenge: they must defeat an opponent in one-to-one combat!"

With a low hum, six bland, dumpy-looking robots descended from the gantries above the stage, moving along columns of bright light. Each one came to a gentle rest next to a finalist robot.

"This," said Master Tronic, rapping his metal knuckles against the helmet-like head of one of the robots, "is a B-class. I designed and built these robots myself. They have only one function, and that is to be beaten up."

The audience laughed and cheered with excitement.

They can't wait for this to start, John thought. His palms were sweating.

"But that doesn't mean it will be easy!" Master Tronic warned. "Each B-class is built to take a lot of punishment, and they remember everything. The more damage you are able to do to them, the more points you will get. But if you manage to damage your own robots, you will lose points."

John looked hard at the squat, barrel-bodied B-class robots. They reminded him of the dummies that martial artists use for practicing kicks and punches.

Master Tronic spread his arms wide. "Each contestant has sixty seconds to attack their B-class opponent," he said. "The robots that do the most damage will go through to the grand final, to face off against one another. As for the others, there is always . . . the Junkyard!"

"Junkyard!" some of the older students yelled, pumping their fists in the air. "Junkyard! Junkyard!"

"Shall we see which of our contestants is up first?" asked Master Tronic.

"YES!" roared the crowd.

John took a deep breath.

Master Tronic opened a panel in his arm, revealing a screen. Characters flickered randomly on it.

"The first robot into the Crater of Destruction is . . . Laserdon!"

Spotlights picked out Kaal in the crowd. He made his way to the front of the stage, looking nervous but determined.

Behind him, John could hear some students asking why the robot was called Laserdon, and

John realized he didn't know, either. *I guess this is the round where we find out,* he thought.

The first B-class waddled into the middle of the crater. With Laserdon perched on his arm, Kaal crouched at the crater's edge. His whole body seemed tense as he waited for the signal to begin.

A soft, synthetic female voice echoed across the crater: "Three. Two. One."

A buzzer sounded. The timer began to count down.

Laserdon's eyes burned with brilliant light. It spread its wings and soared into the air. Kaal hung back, controlling it with his remote pad, sending it in a wide swooping circle around the B-class.

Laserdon's head turned, tracking its target like a hawk.

John watched, completely transfixed, and

a little in awe of Kaal's majestic robot. From Laserdon's eyes came two parallel beams of sizzling light. The lights sliced into the B-class robot's casing, and as Laserdon veered around it, they opened it up like a tin can.

The B-class joggled around in one spot, as if something deep inside it had gone wrong.

Laserdon completed its circle. Then the beams vanished. The upper half of the B-class fell off with a clatter, revealing its tangled wire innards.

Laserdon swept in for the kill and sent a fresh blast of double lasers into the robot's exposed core. There was a flare of blue light like an arc welder, the smell of burning circuits, and an abrupt *bang*.

The smoking, blackened shell of the B-class toppled over and lay still.

Master Tronic came over and carefully

extracted a little black box from the robot's remains.

Kaal looked at it with a worried expression. "Sorry, sir," he said. "I think I might have broken your robot."

The hall exploded with cheers.

John heard someone nearby saying, "They give points based on damage, right? So how many points do you get for blowing it up completely?"

No one seemed to know.

Next up was Charly, the robotic jellyfish. Raytanna had built it to respond to voice commands, but when she started yelling, "Strangle it! Use your tentacles!" in her squeaky voice, the audience burst out laughing. That made Raytanna upset. The more everyone laughed, the more frustrated and angry Raytanna was.

Charly wrapped three of its tentacles around the B-class, squeezing with all its strength. The B-class struggled and exuded a groan of tortured metal, but John didn't think it looked badly damaged at all.

You can't strangle something that doesn't breathe, he thought. *Big mistake, Raytanna.*

Raytanna seemed to realize this at the same time as John — but with only twenty seconds left on the clock.

"Charly! Supernova mode!" she shrieked, jumping up and down.

The roars of laughter from the audience changed to *oohs* of appreciation, as Charly flared up with a sudden surge of energy. A miniature sunburst of rays blasted from the robot, searing and blackening the B-class all over. Smoke began to curl from the crater.

And then the buzzer rang.

Time was up.

John felt sorry for Raytanna as she trudged back to her seat, shoulders sagging.

She lost this round and she knows it! Maybe Super-Rover is in with a chance, after all. . . .

But then John saw Quondass val Haq stomping up to the crater, getting his heavy-duty drill robot, Rocky, ready to attack the next B-class.

There was no question what the audience thought of his chances — as last year's champion, Quondass had the largest fan base of them all, and they led a *boom-boom-crash* chant that shook the floor under John's feet.

The round began.

Rocky's gleaming drill began to spin, faster and faster, whirring in a blur. Quondass playfully backed Rocky up, charged forward, and then hesitated. He turned to the audience, like a gladiator asking the Roman Emperor what the fate of a defeated opponent should be.

The audience was fired up, and everyone roared, "Finish him!"

Rocky's powerful caterpillar tracks churned and the robot shot forward. The drill ground deep into the side of the B-class, tearing away slices of its casing like pencil shavings.

Quondass val Haq punched the air, Rocky snarled and the drill bit deep, the audience whooped and hollered —

And then the drill got stuck.

A grinding screech came from the hapless robot. Quondass wrestled with his remote control, but smoke was already beginning to seethe from beneath Rocky's plating.

The drill bit was stuck fast in the B-class and couldn't turn, and the engine was starting to overload.

It's just like that time Dad's drill got stuck in the wall and tripped the circuit breaker, John thought. Except by the looks of it, Rocky didn't have a circuit breaker. Flames had begun leaping from its back.

The timer buzzed, and Master Tronic quickly ran forward with a fire extinguisher.

Once Quondass had sadly removed Rocky's smoldering remains from the crater, it was Gredilah's turn. Her robot, Fop, shuffled forward, looking absurdly toy-like, its huge grinning head tracking from side to side.

"Hope you put fresh batteries in that thing," John muttered under his breath.

Fop turned out to be just about as dangerous as a toy robot. It stayed far back, firing hissing sprays of sparkling light that seemed to do only a tiny amount of damage. Once or twice the B-class wobbled dramatically and its eyes flashed red, but when the final buzzer sounded, it looked almost completely unhurt.

I guess she built her robot for show, not for fighting, John thought.

Now there were only two contestants left: John and Mordant.

John sat, every muscle tense, waiting to hear who would go next. He could feel Mordant's gaze on him from three rows over, willing him to fail.

"Next contestant: John Riley!"

John's crowd of followers slapped his back and cheered him as he stood up. He stepped up to the stage, grasping his remote control tightly in both hands. His heart was pounding as he lifted Super-Rover and set him down at the crater's edge.

Then he heard the voice counting down.

"Three . . ."

Everything and everyone else in the room seemed to fade away. The cheers became a distant roar, like waves on the sea. John's world shrank to include only him, Super-Rover, and the B-class in front of him.

"Two . . ."

There could be no mercy. He had to destroy it, tear it to little pieces, or everything was lost.

"One!"

John pressed a control button. Super-Rover crouched, ready to spring. A low growl came from his throat. He no longer looked cute.

The buzzer sounded.

Super-Rover bounded in, instantly on the attack. The beronzium teeth went to work on the B-class, tearing and ripping and shredding the metal.

A section of the B-class came loose and John controlled Super-Rover to grab it between his teeth, causing him tug it free like a terrier pulling on a chew toy. He gave the exposed machinery beneath a whack with the razor-sharp tail for good measure. Severed wires sparked and fizzed, and oil spurted out in a black mess.

Fifteen seconds had passed, and the B-class was already looking ragged. Feeling confident now, John sent Super-Rover to chew on the robot's other leg. The teeth chomped down hard, sinking deep — and he could see, as Super-Rover's jaws opened again, that some had been torn out!

John fought to stay calm. *It's okay,* he told himself. *Don't panic, he's not too badly hurt. He still has most of his teeth. And there's always the tail to fall back on.*

Super-Rover bit again, clamping on tight. John waggled a control. The robot shook the B-class without letting go, pulling it crashing down onto its side. John saw that the robot's underside was hardly armored at all, and excitedly he controlled Super-Rover to tear and bite at it, lashing and lashing with its tail.

When the buzzer finally sounded, it was like an alarm clock, waking him up from a very long dream.

The crowd was chanting his name. The mangled wreck of the B-class lay at his feet. Poor Super-Rover wasn't looking much better, with half his teeth missing and a grinding sound coming from his back legs.

He tried to follow John out of the crater, but his legs were moving jerkily and wouldn't carry him. John had to pick him up and hurry back to his place.

A horrible thought crept into his mind and wouldn't go away: *I pushed him too far, and now he's broken. . . .*

"Final contestant: Mordant Talliver!" boomed Master Tronic.

As Mordant took the stage, John saw that he wasn't sneering at the audience. He looked deadly serious — and maybe even a tiny bit nervous.

Mordant set IFI down and stood waiting for the signal, his eyes narrowed in deep concentration.

He's so determined to make it through to the final, John thought. *How's this all going to end? Mordant against Kaal? Kaal against me?* His stomach churned with nerves just thinking about it.

The battle began. IFI's eight arms extended from its middle, and it began to spin around on the spot.

At the ends of those arms, needle guns opened fire, peppering the B-class with high-velocity shot. John instantly saw what Mordant was doing. By keeping IFI spinning, every one of its guns got a chance to fire in turn. Constant bombardment.

"Smart," John said to himself. Mordant might be a jerk, but John had to admit that his robot was pretty slick.

Next, needler bullets ripped into the B-class's body. They didn't do a lot of damage individually, but taken all together, they were shredding it like buckshot. It soon looked more perforated than the edge of a postage stamp. Bits of armor were pinging off the hull and a spreading puddle of oil was beginning to form beneath it.

By the time the final buzzer sounded, the B-class looked like it had been put through a waste disposal shredder. One of its legs was gone, and pieces were hanging off by single cables.

John couldn't guess where he stood in the ranking now. Kaal seemed like the obvious front runner — but who had taken the all-important second place?

"You did great!" his fans assured him excitedly. "You're through to the final, we'd bet on it!"

"Thanks," he said, crossing his fingers. Then a hush fell over the hall as Master Tronic took to the stage again.

"Will the semi-finalists please line up at the front of the stage?"

The six students obediently trooped up in front of the audience.

The B-class robots came waddling out and stood next to them, except for the one Laserdon had completely destroyed. Instead, Master Tronic carefully put its black box down next to Kaal.

"The scores will now be announced, in reverse order."

John suddenly realized the B-class robots' placement on the stage was so that they could announce the scores themselves.

"CHARLY: THIRTEEN POINTS."

"I was afraid of that," said Raytanna with a sigh. "Not enough compensation for the gravometric tolerance inverters. That's pretty obvious in hindsight."

"FOP: TWENTY-ONE POINTS."

Gredilah didn't say anything. She just muttered something unintelligible.

"ROCKY: FIFTY-NINE POINTS."

Quondass val Haq shook a scaly fist in the air, smiling despite his defeat.

"I was bored with winning anyway!" he joked. Loud cheers erupted immediately from the crowd.

"SUPER-ROVER: EIGHTY-SEVEN
POINTS."

Gasps rang out. John felt as if the stage was
giving way beneath him.

*Third place. After everything I've been through, I
only got to lousy third place. I was so close, I nearly
made it! But now Mordant's going to . . .*

"IFI: EIGHTY-SEVEN POINTS."

John's jaw dropped.

NOT third place! Tied for second!

The crowd went absolutely crazy.

"LASERDON: ONE   HUNDRED
POINTS," grated the metallic voice from the
black box.

Master Tronic had to hold up his hands for
calm. Students were jumping up and down on
the spot, hugging each other, waving their arms,
and howling at the top of their voices.

"It seems we have three finalists!" Master

Tronic roared. "Congratulations to each one of you! You must now prepare yourselves for this evening's grand finale. You have six hours to tune up your robots in any way you see fit. You may repair any damage, reprogram any circuits, and strengthen any special abilities. And if you wish to add any last-minute surprises, now is the time to do it!"

"Oh, I will," Mordant Talliver whispered, loud enough for John to hear. "You can bet on it."

As the applause washed over him, John looked down at his battered robot.

He wondered if Super-Rover had any chance at all. Half its teeth were missing and its back legs looked badly out of alignment.

In six hours, whether it was ready or not, that robot was going up against both IFI and Laserdon.

Now John needed to work like he'd never worked before, or Super-Rover wouldn't even last for six *seconds*. . . .

CHAPTER 10

Only a day ago, every desk in the tech lab had been full, as every single student worked on his or her robot. Now, only one of the desks was taken, but the room was far from empty.

Surrounding John was his crowd of eager supporters. John had more than ever, now that some of the defeated semi-final robots' fans had thrown in their lot with him. But the one person John actually wished was there was busy working on Laserdon in the tech lab next door. He'd bumped into Kaal in the corridor moments earlier, but Kaal was busy chatting to his fans about his ideas for possible improvements to Laserdon.

John had even shouted, "Hey!" a few times in desperation to get Kaal's attention, but it seemed he hadn't even noticed. Or if he had, he'd been too preoccupied to reply.

Later today they'd be competing against each other — and against Mordant, of course. It felt wrong.

Kaal was his best friend at Hyperspace High. Kaal had stuck up for him more times than John could remember; he'd helped John get used to the place when he'd first arrived — they even shared a dorm.

What would life be like, he wondered, if this contest ruined their friendship?

"Can one of you pass me the mag-wrench?" he asked his fans, trying to focus on the task in front of him. Instantly it was pressed into his hand. Bracing himself for the worst, John unfastened Super-Rover's armored casing and looked inside.

The damage was even worse than he'd imagined. The servos on Super-Rover's hind legs had shorted out, and the wiring was a blackened, melted mess, like burned spaghetti in a pan.

Fluoron sucked his teeth. "That looks really nasty! Better strip all that out and fit a new motivator unit."

"Perfect opportunity to beef it up a bit!" urged the walrus-creature. "More power, that's what you need!"

"I don't know," John said doubtfully. "I just want to get him working again."

"Don't be stupid!" the walrus-creature yelled. "You want to win, don't you? How's your robot going to snatch Laserdon out of the air without powerful legs?"

John's crowd of supporters agreed that this was an excellent point. They yelled advice and fetched him materials from the Junkyard until his head began to spin and the pile of scrap parts was as high as his desk.

He couldn't shout at them to go away and leave him alone. He just had to work as hard and as fast as he could.

Something's been up with Kaal ever since Robot Warriors began. I don't want to win if winning means losing his friendship, he thought. *I just want Mordant NOT to win. That would be enough.*

But his supporters wouldn't ever understand that.

And he certainly couldn't tell them.

"Where is Mordant?" wondered a squat gray student with huge ears like radar dishes, interrupting John's thoughts. "How come he's not working on his robot?"

"It's already perfect and doesn't need fixing!" someone shouted, mocking Mordant's sneering voice. "Or at least that's what he says. But I saw him tinkering with it in his dorm, putting some new module in."

"Typical!" said Xyglurz with a snort. "Bet you anything he's trying to cheat, and doesn't want anyone to know about it. That slimy . . . Headmaster!"

"What?" John looked up.

A sparkling shape was forming next to him. It could only be Lorem.

All the students fell silent as Lorem materialized into the room, glowing softly as he always did.

"Um, good morning, sir," said John hesitantly.

"Good morning, John," Lorem said. "Congratulations on doing so well in the competition."

"Thank you, sir," John said, wondering if Lorem still thought he'd be happier back on Earth. But the headmaster's face gave away no clue of what he was thinking.

"I won't take up much of your time," Lorem said. "So, this is Super-Rover. How nice to meet him. I hope he wasn't too badly damaged?"

"Actually, he was pretty bashed up. But I'm doing my best to fix him."

"Excellent. I am glad to see you looking after him so well. A good master takes care of his pet. I'm sure he will look after you, too." Lorem's eyes twinkled.

Then he transformed himself into a ball of light and zigzagged between several startled students before vanishing through the floor, leaving John to wonder what he might have meant by his comment.

Before John could ask anyone what they thought Lorem was talking about, Emmie came shouldering her way through the crowd, looking breathless and tousled.

"Hi, John!" she said. "Wow. Getting though your fans is harder than getting through a force field!"

"Your scientific adviser's here," said Fluoron with a laugh, nudging John in the ribs.

"Hi, Emmie!" John said, ignoring him. "Ugh, don't mention force fields. I need some way of getting through IFI's, or Super-Rover will just bounce off."

"Can't help you there," Emmie said, "but just hold still a second. . . ." She lifted a pencil-sized scanner and quickly scanned John up and down with a flickering green ray.

The scanner beeped, then trilled, "Data acquired."

"All done!" Emmie said. "Okay, got to go and talk to Kaal now. See you later. Bye!"

And with that, she plunged back into the crowd.

"What was that all about?" Kritta asked, sounding bemused.

"No idea," John answered, shaking his head. Emmie was acting a little strange, that was for sure, but right now he didn't have time to wonder why.

That mention of force fields was preying on his mind. On a whim, he typed *force field disruptor* into the desk-com, and a design popped up immediately. *Aha! Now I just need to build it. . . .*

"Whose side is she on, anyway?" Fluoron grumbled. "Running off to help Kaal?"

"Good," Xyglurz said, smirking. "I wouldn't

want her on my side. She'll probably do something stupid to that robot of Kaal's."

"She's my friend!" John said angrily. "And she's one of the best pilots in this whole school. Emmie knows more about flying than anyone. So just shut up!"

While John worked, miserable thoughts chased one another through his mind.

It feels like it's all over. Kaal, Emmie, and I were the best of friends the day before yesterday. Now I can't even talk to Kaal, and I don't have a clue what's going on with Emmie. It's like she's hiding something. Some kind of secret. I've got to try to win. I've got to prove an Earth kid can do this! But what if I do win — and I lose my best friend?

If I could just talk to him . . .

John tugged the old servomotor unit out of its blackened cavity. Now he had to fit the new powered-up one, but he wasn't sure how he was supposed to do it. There were at least eleven or twelve different wires to attach, plus a sort of hexagonal spindle. Where was everything supposed to go?

He wished he could ask his best friend. Kaal would know; he loved tinkering with technology. He did this kind of thing for fun.

But right now, it felt like Kaal was a galaxy away.

CHAPTER 11

The rest of the day passed in a blur. It came as a shock when an announcement blared over the ship's sound system:

"This is Master Tronic speaking. Would all students please make their way to the Center, where the grand finale of the Robot Warriors contest will begin shortly!"

One by one, John's fans began fist-bumping, high-fiving, and back-slapping him for luck, wishing him well. They emptied out of the room in a living torrent, excitement at fever pitch.

"Guess I'd better go, too," John said, picking up Super-Rover in both hands.

The souped-up robot felt much heavier than before. That was no wonder, since now he was crammed with extra power cells and a force field disruptor.

One of the Examiners came humming up to John's desk.

"Contestant Riley," it said. "Take your robot and go to your dormitory. Await collection there."

The hallways on the way to the dorm were all deserted, since all the students had already gone to the Center. John had never seen the dorm as empty as this, and he thought it gave the ship a strange, spooky feel, as if Hyperspace High had been abandoned except for him and set adrift in space.

He soon reached his dorm. Finally, a chance

to relax and talk to Kaal away from the crowds, he hoped. He urgently needed to have an honest conversation with his friend before the final started.

John put Super-Rover down at the foot of the bed, lay back, and stared up at the ceiling, waiting for his friend to arrive.

"Come on, you big green geek. I really want to talk to you," he said. "You know I'm still your friend, right?"

The silent room didn't answer. John looked to the door, at the ceiling, and back at the door again.

Come on, Kaal. What's taking you so long?

John stood up, unable to relax. He paced up and down, feeling restless and nervous about the impending contest.

He couldn't understand why Kaal hadn't come back to the dorm, too, and began to wonder if his friend might be avoiding him. But why?

John jumped as the door slid open.

"Hi," said Kaal.

"Hi," John replied.

"So, um, here we are," said Kaal.

"Yes," said John.

Wow, this is incredibly awkward, he thought nervously.

Kaal looked at the wall. John looked at the floor. Seconds ticked past.

Finally on our own, John thought, *and I can't figure out what to say.*

"Good luck," Kaal suddenly burst out. "In the final, you know."

"Oh. Yeah!" John said, forcing a smile. "Good luck to you, too."

Suddenly Emmie leaped into the room with a bundle of white fabric under her arm.

"Yes! I got to you in time!" she said. "Okay, boys, listen up. I was going to make one of these for whoever got to the final, but then you both did, so I had to make two, and that took *forever*. But they're done now, so . . . okay! Here you go!"

She spread two white jumpsuits out on John's bed, one his size, the other Kaal's. The material glimmered with translucent threads, with little pulses of light running through. It reminded John of Emmie's hair.

"It's biofeedback mesh fabric!" she announced proudly. "It keeps your body comfortable, no matter what's happening to you. You'll never be too hot or too cold. Plus you'll look awesome."

"These are amazing!" John said, feeling the soft, shimmering fabric. "I don't know what to say!"

"Thanks, Emmie," Kaal said, sounding emotional. "I — wow. I'd better go and put it on."

"Good luck, both of you," Emmie said. She smiled. "Oops. Time's up. I need to go, so you two can make your grand entrance. See ya! I'll be right in the front row!" With that, she was gone.

John changed into his suit in the bathroom. When he came out, Kaal had disappeared.

But something else was there.

Waiting for John in the doorway was a crimson globe. It was as tall as he was, and it was pulsing with light and completely enveloped by flickering orange flames. The flames gave off no heat — it had to be a holographic trick of some kind.

All the same, John backed away from it, wary.

"Is this what Emmie meant about a grand entrance?" he said to the globe.

The flaming globe hovered patiently on the threshold. John could just make out a small circular platform inside it.

"I'm supposed to step into this thing?" John asked.

It's here to get me, John thought. *Kaal must have had one, too. The final's about to start. I have to get inside.*

He tried to make his legs move. And found that he couldn't.

All he could do was stand there, staring, paralyzed.

He couldn't face it. What was he thinking? He was going to fail, and the whole school would laugh at him, Mordant loudest of all. Although at least then, if he lost, Kaal might be his friend again. . . .

John imagined flying through the ship inside that flaming ball and felt a little sick. He turned away, not wanting to look at it.

Nope. He wasn't going. They couldn't *make* him go. He folded his arms. The red globe would just have to hover there all night.

"Hey, John!" Zepp's voice rang out. "You're meant to get into position inside the globe. Kaal's already heading to the Center in his."

"I figured that out by myself," John said hoarsely. He still didn't move.

"What's wrong? Getting cold feet?"

"To be honest, yeah. I don't think I'm cut out for this after all."

"Really?" said Zepp, sounding as genuinely amazed as a computer could. "You stayed on Hyperspace High when Lorem said you could go home if you wanted, you built a robot although you'd never made one before, you made it through ALL the rounds, all the way to the grand finale, you've got half the school cheering for you . . . and *now* you want to back out?"

John laughed. "Well, when you put it like that, it does sound kind of stupid."

"You'll do fine, John. Trust me on this, will you?"

"Okay, Zepp. I guess I'm just nervous."

"You and every other finalist in the history of Robot Warriors," Zepp said. "Go on. Show them what an Earth boy can do."

John picked up Super-Rover and slowly walked to the door. The globe was silently waiting. He took a deep breath.

"Here goes," he said, and stepped in.

The globe began to spin around him, gathering speed, throwing bright plumes of fire in all directions, bathing the corridor in light.

The next second, it took off down the corridor with blinding speed. Hall lights volleyed past like rounds of laser cannon fire.

John clung to the globe's side with one hand and clutched Super-Rover with the other. He felt giddy and thrilled down to his bones as the corridors and hallways of Hyperspace High became a rollercoaster ride.

John struggled to stay upright as the globe rocketed around corners and past empty classrooms. He almost lost his grip on Super-Rover when they shot around the right-angle turn by the Computer Science rooms. Wouldn't that be something, showing up to the finals without a robot?

John smiled, in spite of himself.

He tried to relax and enjoy the ride, and just about managed it. It was faster and cooler than any fairground ride he'd ever been on.

Excitement began to take over — then, to his horror, he saw that the TravelTube doors up ahead were opening.

And there was no elevator there, only a shaft! As he fell, John braced himself for the inevitable smash far, far below.

CHAPTER 12

The globe shot through the TravelTube doors, but it didn't fall. Instead it flew *up*, rushing past floor after floor like a TravelTube car gone berserk. Open doors were waiting high above, and the globe flung itself out through them.

They shot over a balcony, and suddenly there was no floor below, no walls to the side, no ceiling above.

John was floating in the air, clutching his robot, too amazed to move.

This was the Center. It had to be. But the

bottom half was pitch dark, and the upper half was starlit space. John couldn't see anything below, not the trees, not the cafeteria tables, not even the sparkling lake. Some sort of glowing platform hung in the middle of the huge arena. What was going on?

John tried to figure out what he was seeing. He could hear the crowds roaring below. But above, where the roof usually was, he saw an immense circular opening out onto space. Thousands of brilliant stars shone above him, taking his breath away.

The roof's open! How did they DO that? The atmosphere should be rushing out of the ship, taking everyone with it! It must be some sort of force field or artificial gravity!

As he drew nearer, he got a better look at the platform. It was the size of a skating rink, but with no barriers or walls — no sides at all, in fact. Almost invisible, it hung in the air below the open roof, with no physical struts or girders supporting it.

It glowed faintly, pulsing with blue, and violet luminescence — like it was made simply of light and nothing else, like a digital platform in a computer game.

John noticed a beam of foggy reddish light thrumming up from below, the platform seeming to balance somehow on it like a plate on a juggler's stick.

I get it! he thought. *That must be a manipulator beam, kind of like a giant version of the ones the Examiners use!*

Two more colored flaming globes were approaching the platform, glowing bright against the darkness. The roar of the crowd grew louder and louder.

There, in a green globe wreathed in emerald

and turquoise flames, was Kaal. He was clutching Laserdon, whose wings gleamed with new silver fittings.

Mordant was in the other globe, which was a deep blue. Violet and indigo flames hissed and raged over it, as if it were the eye of some mythical space dragon. They lit Mordant's face from below, making it look skull-like and deeply sinister.

The closer the three globes came to one another, the more fiercely their flames burned.

Emmie was right, John thought. This was the most spectacular entrance he'd ever made in his life!

The globes drew up to the edges of the platform. As his eyes grew accustomed to the dark, John realized the cheering audience was packed tightly into the balconies around the Center. He could just make out Holo-Placards glowing dimly in the dark below, waving like crazy.

John took his cue from Kaal and Mordant and stepped out onto the platform, holding his robot. The cheers were deafening now, bearing them up on an ocean of noise.

Walking on the near-invisible platform was like walking on thin air, and the length of the manipulator beam holding it in place made it clear just how far there was to fall.

Don't think about it, John warned himself. *There's a battle to fight.*

"Welcome, one and all, to the grand finale of Robot Warriors! I'm sure this will be a contest you will remember clearly for the rest of your lives. . . ."

Lorem's voice boomed out from all around, but John couldn't see the headmaster himself anywhere. In fact, it was almost impossible to see *anything*, apart from the platform and his fellow finalists.

This reminded John of the time he performed in the school production of *Oliver!* last year, before he'd come to Hyperspace High. He hadn't been able to see his mom and dad in the audience — or anyone else, for that matter. The bright spotlights shining on the stage had cast everything else in the room in complete and total shadow.

He quickly snapped back to reality. Lorem had just said his name. He forced himself to listen.

"For young John Riley, reaching the final has been a formidable challenge. He is from Earth, a planet few of you will have heard of, though after today I think you may want to find out more about it!"

A ripple of applause ran around the Center.

John grinned. He was feeling proud of his home planet.

"John has never designed a robot before. Few on his home planet have ever owned one. And yet, his unique creation, Super-Rover, has reached the final. As if this were not enough, I remind you all that John has been with us for *less than a full semester,* making his achievement all the more remarkable."

A tremendous wave of applause roared up from the crowd.

John felt a mix of emotion. Lorem's words had left him feeling immensely proud, but he also felt a little bit confused. He couldn't help thinking that if he'd listened to the headmaster's grave doubts earlier on, he wouldn't even be here now.

"As for Kaal Tartaru," Lorem continued, "he has been a credit to this school in many ways. In his first year at Hyperspace High, he has amazed his teachers with his technological ability. However, I would not be surprised if most of you had no idea of this. Not everyone who gets great grades likes to boast about it."

There was a meaningful pause.

"Kaal is one of the most polite, modest students it has ever been my pleasure to have on this ship," Loren went on. "I am sure his family is very proud of him. I know I am."

Once again, there was a surge of applause and cheers.

"Meanwhile, in our final contestant, Mordant Talliver, we see the continuation of a proud family tradition."

A deathly hush fell over the whole Center as Lorem spoke.

John listened intently. Mordant's face was a rigid mask, his jaw clenched, his eyes narrowed as everyone gazed back at him. John had to wonder how Lorem could possibly find anything positive or nice to say about Mordant. The guy was a total jerk.

But what Lorem did say left John completely amazed.

"Mordant, as some of you may know, is not the first Talliver to make it to a Robot Warriors final," Lorem said. "His father won a spectacular victory before most of you were born with his famous robot Skulldozer. I am pleased to say that Skulldozer is still with us. He has spent the last twenty years in a display case in my own office, and I often enjoy taking him for a drive when nobody is looking."

The audience laughed, though Mordant continued to glare.

Lorem went on. "Mordant's grandmother, Skavella, destroyed her opponent's robot in fifteen seconds, winning the final in her last year here. And the very first Robot Warriors contest of all was won by Asterion Talliver, Mordant's great-grandfather!"

Murmurs of surprise ran through the crowd.

The realization came to John like a thunderbolt.

So that's why he wants to win so badly!

John almost felt sorry for Mordant. His whole attitude, the sabotage, the arrogance . . . why, none of it was about Mordant himself after all.

As it turned out, the whole thing was really about Mordant's family. He had a tradition to uphold, and he couldn't afford to fail. If Mordant's father was anywhere near as harsh as his son, John wouldn't want to be in his classmate's shoes.

For the first time, John felt that he understood

Mordant Talliver. The pressure he was under must be unbelievable. If he lost, he'd probably be the first Talliver ever to lose.

"Finally," said Lorem, "I would like to draw your attention to a remarkable fact. For the first time ever in the history of Robot Warriors, our finalists are all first years! So, special congratulations are due to all three of you for making school history before the final has even begun!"

The cheers that followed were the loudest yet. But when Lorem spoke again, sounding gravely serious, they quieted down.

"Contestants, set down your robots," the headmaster said.

John, Kaal, and Mordant obeyed. They looked at one another nervously across the glowing platform, the hopes of the entire school resting on their shoulders.

"This is the final battle," declared Lorem. "There can be no mercy and no escape. The robots must fight each other — to the *death*!"

CHAPTER 13

Like a pair of battle cruisers opening fire on one another, lights suddenly flashed from around the arena. Diamond white, acidic yellow, ruby-laser red, nebula blue, they bombarded the stage with color. Programmed lighting sequences kicked in, and the barrage of light became a firework display, as snakes of rainbow beams chased each other around the arena and burst into luminous fountains.

Then, gradually, the cavalcade of lights slowed.

One by one, they winked out until only three spotlights were left, focusing on John, Mordant, and Kaal.

Those lights went off all at once, and the sudden total darkness was like reality itself being switched off.

The silence was absolute.

John could feel the entire population of the school far beneath him, waiting breathlessly for something to happen, like a single vast living thing.

In the complete silence, John could hear his own heartbeat.

All at once a sudden blast of electronic music sounded, like the opening chord of a wild organ solo. The stage flared with light, a ring of spotlights encircling it like a crown.

That must be the signal for us to begin! This is it — the battle's on!

John didn't think the cheers could get any louder, but they did. They roared up from below like a tidal wave. Kaal and Mordant were already reaching for their remotes, powering up their robots.

John fired up his own remote, his hands trembling. But the cheers that were meant to support him were actually starting to distract him. He was never going to be able to concentrate with all this noise!

I don't have to win, he reminded himself. *It's okay if Kaal wins. I'd be happy for him. I just have to stop Mordant!*

He forced the cheering voices out of his mind.

Focus, John!

He sent Super-Rover charging toward the middle of the stage. IFI was there already, and to John's dismay, the robot already had all eight of its spindly arms out. It spun in place, whizzing like a circular saw. It fired a screaming hail of needler bullets at Super-Rover and Laserdon, both at the same time.

John jammed a control hard to the side, and Super-Rover rolled over to the left, dodging the stream of needlers.

Laserdon wasn't so lucky. The needlers peppered the graceful robot under the wings, blasting him backward and out over the edge of the arena.

The crowd gasped. For a second, John thought Laserdon would plummet all the way down and smash into a million pieces on the ground below.

Then Laserdon quickly recovered and went back on the attack right away, swooping up over the rim.

Mordant didn't miss his chance. IFI zoomed

toward Laserdon, bringing all its guns to bear on the hovering robot.

Another blast like that could rip his wings clean off, John realized. *I have to take the heat off Laserdon!*

John sent Super-Rover in a power charge, slamming into IFI's back. The conical robot wobbled; its spray of bullets completely missing Laserdon.

Time to attack!

John made Super-Rover gnash his teeth and snap at IFI, biting hard with his beronzium teeth.

To John's delight, the force field disruptor was working. Super-Rover grabbed one of IFI's arms and ripped it off in his strong jaws. It went skittering across the platform like a broken umbrella strut.

Mordant howled in rage and trained IFI's guns from Laserdon to Super-Rover. But before he could fire, Kaal let rip with Laserdon's eye-beams.

He boosted the power on those, John thought, watching as the twin lances of laser light scorched IFI.

Ripples of heat clearly outlined IFI's force field.

Was it John's imagination, or was it not as strong as before? Maybe IFI wasn't as invincible as Mordant had thought!

Mordant snarled. IFI opened fire on Super-Rover at point-blank range. There was a noise like stones pinging off a windscreen, as bullets ripped into the robot dog's armor.

John hastily went in for a counter-attack, controlling Super-Rover to grab another of IFI's arms and tug at it.

But this one didn't come off so easily!

Super-Rover pulled and tore at the arm,

dragging IFI like a real Jack Russell terrier playing a game with a stick.

Meanwhile, another bright stab of laser light from behind weakened IFI's force field even more. Kaal was taking advantage of the situation!

"Fight fair!" Mordant yelled furiously.

He spun IFI around, faster and faster, trying to shake off Super-Rover.

But John made him bite down even harder on the arm in his jaws.

Good dog! Hang on! John thought.

As IFI's arms spun, the little robot dog whizzed around in a circle until finally, with a grotesque snap, the arm broke and Super-Rover went skidding helplessly across the platform.

Now IFI was down to six arms, and it seemed to John as if its force field was finally beginning to fail.

Super-Rover lay on his back, his legs jerking. John tried to roll him back onto his feet, but he was hopelessly stuck.

Laserdon swooped in toward him, his eyes glowing bright. John felt his heart leap into his mouth.

Game over! Kaal's got a clear shot at my robot, and there's nothing I can do. . . .

The lasers fired . . .

. . . and sliced right through yet another of IFI's arms, missing Super-Rover completely. Kaal gave John a wink and a grin.

The crowd roared. Mordant looked like he was about to explode.

"Fight each OTHER!" he screamed angrily. "Don't just gang up on me! You're CHEATING!"

IFI fired another volley at Laserdon, but only a few shots connected.

Meanwhile, John desperately tried to get Super-Rover to stand up. Nothing he tried was working.

Suddenly John thought, *There's only one thing I can do.*

He fired the rocket booster — and Super-Rover did a neat flip through the air, landing on all four paws!

Mordant howled miserably. Laserdon had almost stripped IFI's force field now. John grinned and sent Super-Rover in for a fresh attack.

This is more fun than I expected!

Between them, John and Kaal harried IFI into a standstill.

No matter what Mordant did, he couldn't fight them both off at once. He settled for firing some of IFI's guns at each of them, while Super-Rover snapped and lashed with his razor-sharp tail and Laserdon blasted away from above the robot.

I'm not going to win this, John thought. *Laserdon's just too powerful. But at least I'm doing my best. At least my fans seem happy.* They continued to chant his name.

But Mordant was far from happy. IFI looked terrible now. The force field was gone, and the robot's casing was scarred and dented from Super-Rover's constant attacks. Only three needler guns were left. The others were scattered across the arena, chewed or melted off.

The look on Mordant's face said it all. He'd lost and he clearly knew it. All the arrogance had gone.

IFI raised its arms, shaking all over, as if to make one final attack.

John prepared Super-Rover for a dodge. He could see Kaal doing the same with Laserdon.

IFI surely had enough punch left in him to take out one of them. But which one would it be? Whichever robot *didn't* get taken down would immediately finish IFI. And that would make it the winner!

But no one was prepared for what happened next.

"If I don't win," howled Mordant, "then nobody wins!" He jabbed a button on his control pad.

IFI began to tremble. Its force field became visible and shifted through the color spectrum, from violet to green to fiery red. Smoke began to pour through the cracks in its casing.

Mordant threw down his control panel and ran, jumping into his blue globe, sobbing. He had his hands over his ears. The globe began to drift away from the platform.

"Mordant! What are you *doing*?" John yelled.

A chorus of outraged boos and yells came from the crowd.

Suddenly Emmie's panicked voice pierced through the noise. "John! Kaal! Get back! His robot's going to self-destruct!"

IFI was glowing all over now, as its casing grew hotter and hotter. A hissing sound was coming from it, and the sound was growing louder.

Time seemed to slow down. John turned and tried to run toward his globe, toward safety. He took one step — and then the explosion came.

The shockwave flung him painfully to the ground. Kaal was sprawling, too. The entire platform lurched beneath them.

A fragment of IFI landed on his arm and stuck there, sizzling like an ember. John quickly shook it off, glad for the jumpsuit Emmie had made him.

Was the battle over?

He had no idea.

Then he saw Laserdon, lying on the platform next to Kaal. The force of IFI's explosion must have hurled it out of the sky. And there was Super-Rover, battered but still intact.

Kaal's face was twisted in horror, and John quickly understood why. Something was horribly wrong. The platform was still swaying beneath them.

And it seemed to be getting worse.

Kaal was crouching down, hanging on as best he could. "The manipulator beam!" he shouted. "It must have destabilized from the force of the explosion!"

John saw the faint red beam flickering, and he knew that Kaal was right.

"He must have used an electromagnetic pulse," Kaal said, gasping. "It was supposed to destroy all three robots at once, but it crippled the beam, too!"

John gulped. Any second now, the platform would drop like a stone. There had to be some safety system . . . right? Surely the Examiners would catch them, or a force field would activate, or . . .

The platform lurched violently. With eyes shut tight, John braced himself for the drop.

But the drop never came.

Instead, John felt strangely light.

He opened his eyes again, and to his amazement he saw that the whole platform was drifting *upward*.

What was going on? Quickly John realized that he had been wrong about the manipulator beam — it had not been keeping the platform *up*.

It had been holding it *down*.

John, Kaal, Super-Rover, and Laserdon lay sprawled on the great transparent disc. John and Kaal traded horrified looks as they began floating past the very highest of the balconies, through the wide-open roof of the Center, and out toward the stars.

Out to the empty, infinite void of space . . .

CHAPTER 14

John and Kaal hurried toward each other across the rising platform. John realized that his steps were turning into great bounding leaps as he walked.

"We're moving out of artificial-gravity range!" Kaal yelled. "This is really bad, John!"

John looked down. They were outside the ship now.

Don't scream, he told himself. *It's going to be okay. I don't know how, but it is. . . .*

The cheering had stopped. Instead, screams

and yells were coming from the shadowed crowd inside the ship.

"That idiot!" Kaal said despairingly. "I can't believe he's such a poor loser. They'll expel him for sure."

"I'm not worried about him. I'm worried about us!" John said, his voice catching in his throat — it was getting harder to breathe. His breath was forming misty clouds in the pitch darkness.

If it weren't for Emmie's suits, he thought, *we'd be freezing to death.*

From the depths of the ship, Master Tronic's voice rang out: "Just stay calm, boys. Help is coming. We will rescue you."

"S-stay c-calm?" John stammered. "Easy for him to say! He's not the one floating off into outer space!"

Kaal looked around at the starry emptiness

surrounding them. "Okay," Kaal said. "The good news is we're not in outer space. We're in an atmosphere field."

"Is that good?" John asked. "I don't really know what it is."

Kaal laughed. "Yes, it's good. The atmosphere field is used for carrying out repairs, since it's way easier than using spacesuits. With so many different-shaped students on board, we'd need to carry hundreds of different suits anyway —"

"So what's the bad news?" John nearly shrieked. The open ceiling of the Center was a dark circle far beneath them now.

"The bad news is, uh, that we appear to be drifting *out* of the atmosphere field," Kaal said nervously.

"Won't we just slow down?" John asked hopefully.

"Not in zero gravity!" Kaal explained. "Once you start moving, you just keep going in the same direction! Unless something else happens to you."

They looked through the transparent platform down at the ship, which was getting farther and farther away.

John couldn't hear the crowd anymore. He might be protected from the cold, but the air was getting thinner all the time.

His worst nightmare had finally come true. Ejected into space without a spacesuit, and no way to get back!

"Wait!" he yelled. "You've got wings, Kaal! And there's atmosphere out here — so that means you can fly!"

"I can *try*," Kaal said grimly. "We're going to have to jump off this platform, though. Are you cool with that?"

"We haven't got a choice." John put Super-Rover under his arm and climbed quickly onto Kaal's shoulders. "Come on, buddy. Let's do this."

Despite the desperate situation, John felt a surge of relief that his friendship with Kaal seemed to be back on track. This was the most they'd spoken to each other in days! He just hoped they would be able to stay within range of the school's communication system — otherwise they wouldn't be able to understand each other.

Kaal clambered to the edge of the platform, took a deep breath, and launched himself off. His huge wings spread like sails, opening against the thinning atmosphere, struggling as hard as they could to propel the boys back toward the waiting ship.

John glanced back over his shoulder. The

platform sailed off into the darkness of space, with the hapless Laserdon still sitting on it, abandoned.

There was a shimmer as the platform passed through the edge of the atmospheric field. Then it just drifted away, silently spinning into eternity.

Laserdon shrank to the size of a speck of dust, then vanished.

John could feel Kaal's bellow-like lungs heaving as he strained to fly farther. They hardly seemed to be making any progress at all.

"Good thing you can fly," John said, patting his friend on the shoulder and trying to sound cheerful. "We'll be back at the ship in no time! Right?"

"I . . . wish . . . it were that simple!" Kaal said, gasping.

"You mean it's not?"

"We're still moving away from the ship . . . "
Kaal explained. "I'm slowing us down, but not
enough! And look!"

Kaal pointed at the huge engines at the rear
of Hyperspace High. They were blazing with
power.

"Ship's still moving," Kaal whcczcd.
"Leaving . . . us . . . behind."

"What?" John yelled, too horrified to think
straight. "WHY?"

"Everyone . . . was watching . . . the contest!"
Kaal said between gasps for air. "Ship's on
autopilot!"

"Oh, *no!*"

John's breath came in raw, straining gasps as
they drew closer and closer to the field's edge.
He sounded as if he were having an asthma
attack. "I know Zepp can override it, but it'll
take time. . . ."

Kaal's muscles strained as he fought to make headway, but John could tell they were doomed. He could see the entire length of Hyperspace High now, a hulking white shape ahead of them, so close, but so far away.

"We don't *have* time!" John groaned. His chest was in agony.

"I'm sorry, John," Kaal said, sounding almost spent. "I'm trying as hard as I can. It's been . . . an honor. . . ."

John looked down at Super-Rover under his arm.

Stupid. Why did I hang onto this? It's just added weight for Kaal to carry!

"I'm going to throw Super-Rover behind us as hard as I can," John told Kaal. "Action and reaction, right? It might help."

"Good thinking . . . no! Wait!" Kaal said. Suddenly, he sounded almost excited. "Didn't you build a homing system into Super-Rover when you designed him?"

"Yes!" John shouted. "Kaal, you're a genius! One press of a button, and he'll whoosh us right back to the tech lab! Wait a second, where's the remote?"

"You're asking ME? I don't have it!" Kaal said. "You're the one who should have it!"

John felt sick. Had the remote gone tumbling into space?

He patted his pockets. To his relief, it was still there. He wrestled it out.

"Hold on tight!" he said, grinning. "Super-Rover, take us home!"

He held his breath and pressed the homing button.

Click.

They waited.

The ship retreated farther into the distance.

John was starting to feel dizzy and light-headed from lack of oxygen. Any moment now, they would drift out of the atmosphere field completely.

Click. Click. Click.

John kept jabbing the button, but nothing happened.

"We're doomed," Kaal said, his voice hollow with despair. "Our only chance of survival is if a rescue craft picks us up before we drift out of the field!"

John forced himself to stay calm. He turned Super-Rover around in his hands, trying to see why the robot dog wasn't working properly. Little pockmarks covered the robot, the marks of Mordant Talliver's needler bullets. John felt angry seeing the wounds. Some of them must have punched through to Super-Rover's inner workings.

"I'll keep us inside the field for as long as I can," Kaal said, wheezing loudly. "Get your robot open. We'll have to try to fix him manually."

I need both hands for this, John thought.

He clamped his legs tight around Kaal's heaving shoulders and fumbled open Super-Rover's body casing. He instantly lost his grip on the cover and it went tumbling end over end into space.

Easy does it, John! he cautioned himself, clutching the robot before it drifted off.

"Find the homing device," Kaal's voice rasped.

John's fingers explored the masses of wires inside the robot.

There *was* damage — and lots of it. Some of the circuit boards had holes the size of postage stamps.

Please, he thought, *please let the homing device be intact!*

It felt like hours had passed, though it could only have been seconds, when John's fingers finally closed on a smooth black cylinder. That was the homing device — he remembered installing it. And by the feel of it, it was still in one piece!

"Got it!" he said.

But there was no switch, so how could he work it if it wasn't able to respond to the remote control?

"Hurry up," Kaal said, sounding choked. "Running out of air . . ."

"It's not working!"

"Must be a broken connection . . . look for a loose wire. . . ."

John struggled to remember the wiring diagrams he'd worked from. His ears were ringing and his head felt like it was full of prickly cotton.

Then he saw it — one of the power wires had been sliced in two by a stray bullet.

Praying this would work, he twisted the exposed metal ends back together, crossed his fingers, then pressed the control again.

Super-Rover began to hum. His ears twitched.

He's finding the path home!

"I think it might work, Kaal!" John said.

"I hope so," Kaal said, gasping.

Fighting the urge to celebrate their safety too soon, John held Super-Rover tightly under his arm.

"Here goes nothing!"

John pressed the button to fire Super-Rover's rocket booster. The jets fired, and the robot grew hot under his arm.

He was really struggling to breathe now. Beneath him, Kaal's breaths sounded strangled. All they could do was wait. . . .

CHAPTER 15

John didn't let himself believe they were moving faster at first.

Did a tiny little robot like Super-Rover really have the power to carry both him and the huge hulking figure of Kaal back to Hyperspace High? He squeezed his eyes shut for a moment, trying to push down the panic inside his belly as they waited to find out their fate.

Hearing only the whoosh of the space air around him, John realized that Kaal had become deadly silent.

Is he even breathing? John wondered. *Is it too late?*

A sudden shout made John almost lose his grip on his friend.

"We're moving!" Kaal cried out. "Whatever you did, it worked!"

It was true, John saw, as he opened his eyes. They were inching ever so slightly closer to Hyperspace High.

Kaal spread his wings wider, and John held Super-Rover tight. Gradually they built up speed. Super-Rover's antennae ears twitched — he must be busily tracking down his homing signal!

"Come on, little guy!" John told the robot. "Don't let me down now!"

The rocket boosters on Super-Rover's sides changed direction and the jets suddenly blasted at full force.

"He's got it!" John told Kaal in delight. "He's locked on!"

The ship loomed up ahead of them. They were rushing toward it now, like a meteor about to slam into the hull.

John took a deep breath, filling his lungs with delicious, oxygen-rich air.

There was the open ceiling of the Center, straight ahead! But it wasn't dark like before. All the lights were on, and John could see the crowds of students packed into the balconies and stands. Super-Rover put on yet another burst of speed.

"He did it," Kaal said, his voice quiet in wonderment. "That's a strong homing device you've given him! We're heading right for the opening!"

"Listen," John said. "Can you hear cheering?"

The open ceiling gaped in front of them now like the opening of a tunnel. John felt blessed relief washing over him. The crowd of students was jumping up and down, waving their arms, cheering at the tops of their voices.

"Good thing your robot knows how to get inside the ship!" Kaal joked. Then his voice turned serious again. "Uh-oh. John, I just thought of something. Something really important."

"What's the matter? We're almost back at the Center!" John said. He hugged Super-Rover tightly with gratitude. "Look, Kaal! We're home safe!"

They were passing back through the open ceiling of the Center now. Below them lay the huge open arena, ringed by crowds.

"But once we're inside the ship, we'll be in range of the artificial gravity!"

John realized what Kaal meant, seconds too late. "Oh nooooo . . ."

Super-Rover rushed into Hyperspace High, with John still clinging to him, and Kaal clinging to John.

The second they crossed the ship's boundary, two things happened.

First, the ceiling spiraled shut like a colossal iris valve, sealing away the view of space.

Master Tronic yelled, "Incredible! They're safe!"

Next, John, Kaal, and Super-Rover dropped like ten-ton weights, yelling as they fell.

Time seemed to slow down. John felt Kaal grab his arms. Super-Rover fell from his grip. Wind went rushing by, and the faces of hundreds of horrified students shot past his eyes. There was a *whump* as Kaal's wings opened up like a huge parachute.

Then John fell right out of Kaal's exhausted grasp.

John heard a splash and a loud fizzling crackle, like something frying in a pan, as Super-Rover plunged into the lake seconds ahead of them. Then everything was suddenly green, wet, echoey, and very cold.

I hit the Center's lake, he thought.

Something had a grip on him. He was being lifted out of the water.

Stunned and dripping, he felt himself gently floating through the air and being set down on the edge of the lake. The grip belonged to an Examiner, he now saw, holding him in its red manipulator beam.

"I've never been so glad to see an Examiner in my life!" John sputtered.

Beside him, Kaal slapped his back and burst out laughing. The crowd cheered like they would never stop. Hundreds of students came stampeding toward them, climbing down from the balconies and forming a ring around the two students.

The Examiner's beam fetched something else out of the lake next. It took John a couple of seconds to recognize it. It was the waterlogged robot dog that had saved their lives.

Without his casing, and with all his parts exposed, the little robot dog looked pretty pathetic.

John reached out for it and then hesitated as he saw what was happening.

Blue electrical sparks shot out of Super-Rover, and his whole body juddered. His circuits were obviously failing, being shorted out by the water.

The tail wagged once, weakly, and then lay still.

"I think it's game over for Super-Rover," John said with a heavy sigh.

"He died saving us," Kaal said. "That's the most heroic thing I've ever heard of a robot doing."

"Stand aside!" shouted a female voice from beyond the crowd. "Come on, move! Give them some room!"

The next moment, a group of five white robots with flashing blue lights on their heads came rushing through the crowd. Each one had slender arms that divided into dozens of slimmer, more delicate ones, tipped with medical instruments. On their chests were insignia like flaming fireballs. Behind them strode Dr. Kasaria, metallic-skinned and dark-eyed, looking very stern.

"It's the Meteor Medics!" a student's voice yelled.

"Hold still for scanning," Dr. Kasaria snapped, shining a bright beam into John's face. "Hmmm. Skeleton undamaged," she said. "Internal organs functioning normally. Body temperature normal. That's odd."

"My friend made me a special suit," John explained, suddenly feeling very woozy and giddy.

"You appear to be suffering from mild oxygen deprivation," said the ship's doctor. "I'm having you taken to the medical wing immediately. Please relax."

Relax?

John barely had time to shout, "Whoa!" before an invisible force gripped his whole body and tilted him gently backward.

The next thing he knew, he was gliding through the Center on an invisible stretcher held between two of the Meteor Medics. Kaal looked over at him from his own stretcher and gave him a thumbs-up.

The crowd of students surged after them, yelling encouragement and trying to follow the medics, but Master Tronic stepped in front of them and held up his hands.

"Let the Meteor Medics handle it!" he boomed. "There'll be plenty of time to check on them later."

"So who won?" a student yelled from somewhere in the crowd.

John had to smile. Right now, he was just glad to still be alive. Winning was the last thing on his mind.

CHAPTER 16

The medical wing was at the very top of Hyperspace High.

John didn't much like hospitals back on Earth — they seemed to be all yucky disinfectant smells and cabbage-green walls.

But this hospital was astonishing; a maze of dazzling white rooms where hexagonal windows showed spectacular views out over the ship and into space.

The surfaces were so clean, they seemed to glow. Bubbling vats of fluid, big enough to hold a whole person, stood waiting in side rooms. John glimpsed a section called MAJOR SURGERY, where a cluster of laser scalpels hung from the ceiling on robotic arms.

John glided past a sequence of strange mirrored panels that showed his reflection overlaid with what was inside; his muscles, then his skeleton, then his internal organs. For a second, he saw his own heart beating inside his ribs.

"I'm not sure if that's the coolest thing ever or the grossest!" he told Kaal. At least he seemed to be in good working order.

Dr. Kasaria accompanied them to a ward room. Two freshly made beds sat side by side, next to banks of monitoring equipment.

As the Meteor Medics lowered John and Kaal gently onto their beds, the mattresses made a slurping noise and morphed themselves into new shapes, adapting themselves to their exact height and weight.

For a hospital, John thought, *this is pretty luxurious!*

Dr. Kasaria checked the readouts and narrowed her enormous black eyes. "Hmmm. There doesn't seem to be anything seriously wrong with either of you, but we're going to keep you under close observation overnight, just to make sure."

"Can we have visitors?" John asked quickly, thinking of Emmie.

"What you two need most of all is peace and quiet," Dr. Kasaria said, firmly but kindly. "No visitors."

When she was gone, John and Kaal lay side by side in their beds, talking and joking. The time passed quickly without John even noticing. Finally, he could have a normal conversation once again with his best friend. It was just like being back in the dorm, before any of this Robot Warriors stuff had happened.

After a while, they just sat and looked out into space, through the huge window at the end of the room.

"Space looks a lot nicer from in here, doesn't it?" Kaal said.

"Yeah, it does," John agreed. "And it's easier to enjoy the view when you're not gasping for breath."

"So . . ." Kaal seemed to be struggling to find the words. "John, we're still best friends, right?"

"Of course we are!" John said. He laughed. "That is, I mean, if you still want to be best friends."

"Why wouldn't I?" Kaal laughed, too. "Wow. I'm so glad we're still . . . you know. I thought after the competition was over, you wouldn't want to be my friend anymore."

"Are you crazy?" John said, sitting up. "Why would I ever want to stop being friends with you?"

"I thought, if I beat you, you'd think I was on Mordant's side, or something . . . like I thought you weren't good enough to be here." Kaal looked miserable.

John shook his head. "Kaal, I didn't mind losing if it meant *you* got to win," he explained. "I just didn't want Mordant to!" He smiled and said, "You know something? All through this contest, I was worried *you* wouldn't want to be friends with *me*!"

"Well, that settles it," Kaal said solemnly. "We both need to go and have a brain scan right now. Call Dr. Kasaria. Neither of us is right in the head."

They laughed for a long time.

"Oh well," John said eventually. "I guess there was no winner in the end."

Kaal shrugged. "That's fine with me. Mordant lost. He blew his own robot to bits in front of the whole school. I think that counts as a win for everyone."

John hesitated. "You know, when he blew up IFI and it sent the platform floating off into space . . ."

"Yes?"

"Do you think he meant for that to happen?" John asked quietly.

Kaal frowned. "Talliver's a nasty piece of work," he said slowly. "And we all know he hates to lose. But is he really evil enough to try to kill us both?"

"That's what I'm wondering."

"I don't know," Kaal said. "I don't *think* so.

But deep down, I'm really not sure. And that worries me."

"Me, too," John said, with a cold shudder.

CHAPTER 17

"Home, sweet home," John said, sighing as the door to their dorm slid open.

The room was still a mess from the day before. Empty snack bags and food wrappers, drinking cups, and placards lay all over the room.

"It's empty," Kaal said, with a sigh of relief. "Thank goodness. I thought our fans might be hiding in here."

"Maybe we should check under the beds?" John joked.

After he and Kaal had been discharged from the medical wing that morning, he'd half-expected a crowd to be waiting for them. He hoped now that Robot Warriors was over, their supporters had found something else to occupy their time.

"I guess we have to get used to not being famous anymore," Kaal said with a grin. "I can live with that!"

"Welcome back!" Zepp said, his voice ringing from the hidden speakers. "Sorry to interrupt the homecoming, but all students are being called to the main lecture hall. Lorem's called a special assembly; it's due to start in ten minutes."

"Well," John said as they headed straight back out again, "that explains where everyone is!"

When they arrived in the lecture hall, they

saw Emmie waving wildly to them from across the large room.

"She looks like she'll explode if she doesn't get to tell us whatever's on her mind," John said. "Come on!" He and Kaal hurried over and took their places in MorphSeats on either side of Emmie.

"Guess who I saw being dragged off by four Examiners last night?" Emmie burst out, like a Brucko juice foaming over a cup. "Only the biggest loser on Hyperspace High!"

"No way!" John said.

"Yep. Mordant Talliver!" Emmie said proudly.

"That's it, then," Kaal said in wonderment. "He's finished."

"He says he never meant to blow up his robot," Emmie interrupted. "According to *him*, IFI was supposed to go into mega-force-field mode and become completely invulnerable. He says he left the stage because there was no way either of you could win."

"What?" John said in disbelief. "That's total garbage! He tried to blow up all our robots at once!"

"Conveniently, IFI's in a million pieces now," Emmie went on, "so nobody can prove Mordant was lying."

"The Examiners will never believe that!" John scoffed. Then he frowned. "Will they?"

"Well . . ." Emmie frowned. "Mordant was at breakfast this morning, so I guess he hasn't been expelled. But I heard he got a week of detention, and Master Tronic's giving him a fail for technology class. That will *sting*."

"The Examiners probably think *he* believes his story," Kaal said. "He can be pretty convincing."

"You don't think he tried to send you into space on purpose, do you?" Emmie asked nervously.

"I've been thinking about that a lot," John admitted. "You know, I don't think he really meant to do it. When he left the stage, he looked more ashamed than anything."

Kaal nodded. "Ashamed of being the first Talliver to ever lose a Robot Warriors final in the whole history of Hyperspace High."

"Yeah. He knew he was going to lose, and he couldn't face it. So he tried to blow up all the robots out of spite. Remember? '*If I don't win, then nobody wins!*'" John mimicked.

"Talk about being a bad loser," Kaal grumbled. "He nearly got us both killed with that stunt."

"Shhhh!" Emmie whispered. "It's Lorem!"

The headmaster appeared on stage in a

brief shimmer of light. Immediately, the lecture hall fell into a respectful hush.

"I don't need to remind you all what happened yesterday," Lorem said gravely. "You were all there. You all saw what happened for yourselves. I am glad to tell you, however, that nobody was hurt and school will soon continue as normal. I am very grateful to all my staff for their help, especially the Meteor Medics. And now, I believe Mordant Talliver has some words to say."

In front of everyone, Mordant stood up. He stared at the printout in his hand and refused to meet anyone's eye.

"I would (*mumble*) to apolo— (*mumble*) . . ."

"Louder, please," Lorem said cheerily.

Mordant bared his teeth and cleared his throat. "I would like to apologize to John Riley and Kaal in front of the whole school for my appalling behavior during the Robot Warriors final." He took a breath. "I acted in an unsportsmanlike fashion, in opposition to the values of Hyperspace High. I am very sorry and I promise to do better in the future." He sat down heavily.

John and Kaal exchanged glances — and grins.

"Well said, Mr. Talliver. And now, I must point out that the winner of Robot Warriors was never announced."

"What?" John whispered. "I thought there wasn't going to be any winner this year!"

"Me too!" Kaal whispered back.

"I am aware that the outcome of the final was . . . unusual," Lorem said, his eyes twinkling. "But this is a contest, and *someone* has to win. It is a very great honor to be the Robot Warriors champion, and it would be wrong to deny that honor to a deserving winner. So, Master Tronic, if you would?"

Master Tronic's robotic form stepped onto the stage.

"We have reviewed holo-vids of the final battle up to the . . . unfortunate incident," he said. "We decided to award the grand prize to the contestant who scored the most points before the incident took place. And the winner is . . ."

The whole school held its breath.

"Kaal!"

From the applause and cheers, John thought, *you'd think Kaal had saved the entire school from being dragged into a black hole.*

Kaal looked at John, his eyes wide, clearly at a loss for what to do next.

"Get on the stage!" John urged him. The other students agreed, nudging and encouraging him until he eventually stood up and made his way forward. The applause got even louder.

Kaal stood nervously at the front of the stage, licking his sharp teeth. A tiny robotic microphone zipped out of nowhere and hovered in the air in front of him. Moments passed, and nothing happened.

Lorem crossed the stage and laid his hand on Kaal's shoulder. "It is traditional to give a short acceptance speech," he said softly. "A few words will do."

Kaal nodded and took a deep breath.

"I want to say something," he began.

"Yay, Kaal!" yelled a voice from the crowd.

There were some laughs and a little applause.

"I shouldn't be up here," Kaal said in a quiet, clear voice.

The laughter stopped.

"I was proud of Laserdon, but he's nothing

next to John's robot. If it hadn't been for Super-Rover, neither of us would be here at all. We'd be floating out there in space."

The crowd stared up at Kaal in total silence, open-mouthed.

"John's robot saved our lives and brought us back home. No robot has ever done something as cool as that before. So, uh . . . John should be the winner. Instead of me. That's all."

CHAPTER 18

"This is unprecedented!" Master Tronic said. John couldn't tell if he was angry, upset, or just bewildered. "After everything else that's happened, the winner wants to give up his victory! Headmaster, what are we supposed to do now?"

"I suggest you refer to the Examiners," Lorem said, with the hint of a smile. "The Examiners know the rules better than any of us, after all."

"Very well," Master Tronic said slowly, as if

the idea made his circuits crawl. "Could I please have an Examiner on stage?"

Immediately, a panel slid open in a side wall, revealing a waiting Examiner. It glided up onto the stage, humming softly. Kaal stood his ground as it glowered at him.

"A championship victory is not transferable," it said coldly.

"That settles that, then," Master Tronic said. "Now maybe we can —"

"However," the Examiner continued, "according to the competition rules section eighteen point three, subsection delta blue, a championship victory . . . may be shared."

"What do you think, Kaal?" Lorem asked. "Would that work? Would you like to share the victory with John?"

"Yes!" said Kaal, beaming.

"Then, to my great relief," boomed Master

Tronic, "I declare John Riley and Kaal Tartaru joint winners of this year's Robot Warriors contest! John, please join us on the stage!"

Cheers rang out as John made his way through the crowd and joined Kaal on the winner's pedestal in front of Master Tronic.

The robotic teacher presented them with a trophy, shaped like Master Tronic in miniature. It even had a flashing red beam on its little metal skull.

John and Kaal each took one side of the trophy and lifted it together. The applause seemed to go on forever.

John heard Emmie cheering louder than anyone else, and saw her jumping up and down on top of her seat. He never wanted the moment to end.

Eventually, Master Tronic had to quiet the crowd so he could speak again. "History has been made today," he said. "This is the first time there have ever been joint champions in the history of Robot Warriors."

Lorem came across the stage to congratulate Kaal and John and to shake their hands. He gave John a long, steady look, as if his wise old eyes could see into John's soul.

"Congratulations to you, John. Others from more advanced worlds may have called you a primitive Earthling, but you proved yourself their equal, and more. You have showed everyone — especially yourself — that what matters in life is not where you come from, but how far you travel."

John had a sudden thought.

Maybe, when Lorem had offered him the chance to leave Hyperspace High, he'd just been tricking him into trying his very best. After all, why had he felt so determined to prove himself? It had all begun with Lorem's words in the TravelTube. . . .

"Your prize is waiting for you in your dorm room," Lorem said.

With so many happy fans surrounding them, getting back to the dorm room wasn't easy.

Eventually, Emmie stepped in. Hands on her hips, she declared, "Okay, everybody, go carry on the party somewhere else! John and Kaal need a little time to themselves!"

With only a little grumbling, the fans left them alone.

Waiting in John and Kaal's dorm was an amazing device. It looked like a black pedestal ringed with green light, connected by glowing cables to a massive assortment of game controllers — steering wheels, laser sword hilts, joysticks, blaster pistols, and even total-surround helmets.

"Is that what I think it is?" John asked.

Kaal nodded. "John, this is a brand-new HyperDominator 9000 gaming console, with all the peripherals and the virtual-reality add-on pack!"

"Best. Prize. Ever!" They both rushed to the console and began looking through the controllers and game data crystals.

"So," Kaal asked. "Should we play a game or two?"

John grinned. "Why not?"

After all, a bit of healthy competition wasn't going to spoil his relationship with his best friend. He knew that now, for certain.

"Excuse me, John!" Zepp called out. "You have an incoming video call from your parents. Shall I put it through?"

Kaal quickly ducked into his bed pod, out of view.

"Go for it!" said John.

John's parents appeared on the screen, waving. They were sitting on the sofa — the webcam must be next to the TV, John realized. The next moment, a brown and white Jack Russell charged across the screen. He stopped in the middle, cocked his head, and then shot off around the sofa.

"This is the newest member of the family!" John's mom said, laughing.

"As you can see," John's dad said, "he's a lively little guy. Come on, boy! Where's your ball? Where is it?" The Jack Russell wagged his tail and barked as he did another wall-of-death circuit of the sofa.

"He's awesome!" John said.

"I think your dad's in love," his mom said. "He's not sleeping on our bed, though. That's final!"

His dad leaned into the camera, hands on his knees. "So, come on. Don't leave us in suspense. How did you do?"

John frowned. "How did I do?" he asked. "What do you mean?"

"In the competition, of course!" his dad said, smiling.

John's jaw dropped. How could his parents possibly know about Robot Warriors?

"The *science* competition?" his mom prompted him.

Oh, yes! He'd forgotten about the lie he'd told them.

"My project tied for first prize!" he announced proudly.

"That's wonderful news!" his mom said.

His dad clapped. "Great job, kid. I knew that new school of yours would bring out the best in you."

John glanced at his prize. He couldn't wait to try out the new console. "I better go."

"Of course," said his mom. "But before you do, there's one last thing we need to ask you. We can't think of a name for the dog! What do you think we should call him?"

John didn't even hesitate.

"Super-Rover!"

READ THEM ALL!

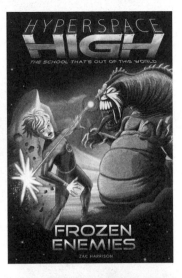

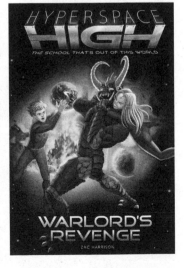